# SNOW
## FALLS

# GERRI HILL

## Bella
### BOOKS
### 2012

Bella Books, Inc.
P.O. Box 10543
Tallahassee, FL 32302

Printed in the United States of America on acid-free paper
First published 2012

Editor: Medora McDougall
Cover Designer: Linda Callaghan

ISBN 13: 978-1-59493-316-5

## Other Bella Books by Gerri Hill

*One Summer Night*
*Gulf Breeze*
*Sierra City*
*Dawn Of Change*
*Artist's Dream*
*Coyote Sky*
*Killing Room, The*
*Behind The Pine Curtain*
*Cottage, The*
*Target, The*
*Rainbow Cedar, The*
*No Strings*
*Scorpion, The*
*Love Waits*
*Storms*
*Keepers of the Cave*

### Hunter Series:
*Hunter's Way*
*In the Name of the Father*
*Partners*

### Mystery Series:
*Devil's Rock*
*Hell's Highway*

## About the Author

Gerri Hill has twenty-two published works, including the 2012 GCLS winner *Hell's Highway* and 2011 GCLS winner *Devil's Rock* and 2009 GCLS winner *Partners*, the last book in the popular Hunter Series, as well as 2012 Lambda finalist *Storms*. She began writing lesbian romance as a way to pass the time while snowed in one winter in the mountains of Colorado. Her first published work came in 2000 with *One Summer Night*. Hill's love of nature and of being outdoors usually makes its way into her stories as her characters often find themselves in beautiful natural settings. Gerri and her longtime partner, Diane, live in the East Texas woods with two Australian shepherds and an assortment of furry felines. For more, see her website: *www.gerrihill.com*.

# CHAPTER ONE

She turned in a circle, hands held out as she sunk past her knees in the fresh snow. The snow clouds had drifted lower, but up here on the mountain, the sun was shining brightly, the blue azure sky almost an overload to her senses. Two feet of fresh snow. Amazing.

"It doesn't get any better than this, girls."

The two Siberian huskies, with their intelligent blue eyes as striking as the Colorado sky, burrowed in the snow around her. She laughed as Kia lunged at Sierra, only to sink to her belly as Sierra jumped safely out of the way.

She paused to watch them frolic, a smile fixed to her face. When Nico had died, she'd decided not to get another. It was heartbreaking to lose him, even though he'd only been with her six years. But as much as she relished the recluse tag that still clung to her, she missed the companionship. A rescue shelter in Denver found her these two, both under a year old. They were a handful at first, so full of energy and childlike joy to be up here in the mountains. Now that their second winter together was underway, she'd adjusted to them. And they to her.

She glanced up the mountain toward Cooper's Peak. It looked heavy with snow, but she'd not lived here long enough to know the mountain yet. After almost six years in Aspen, holed up in a remodeled mining shack outside of town, she'd felt the need to get even farther away from crowds. Especially after running into her brother, of all people, when he brought his entourage up to party and ski.

Hinsdale County—the least populated in all of Colorado—seemed perfect for her. A trip to the tiny town of Lake City confirmed it, and she purchased her property four years ago. Building the cabin proved to be a two-year effort, but she didn't have to rely on anyone up here. Her solar panels and water well gave her all the comforts she needed.

She'd made the mistake of taking too many trips into Lake City, however. Burgers at Sloan's Bar had become a treat, and she'd actually made friends, something she hadn't done in ten years. Reese Daniels, the local sheriff, and her partner Morgan, head of the forest service's regional office here. They were a few years older than she was, but had become her closest friends and were slowly dragging her out of her hermit ways. She shook her head. She even had a satellite dish and Internet now. What kind of a hermit was that?

The test came when she told them who she really was. She'd agonized over it for weeks. Would they treat her differently when they found out her family name? Would they be full of questions? After all, all of that happened ten years ago. But Morgan had drawn her out of her shell, and Reese was like the big sister she never had. So one warm sunny afternoon last summer, over grilled steaks on their back deck, she told them.

"Catherine Ryan-Barrett."

"Who?" Reese had asked.

Morgan had nearly spit her beer out. "Are you *kidding* me?"

"*Who*?" Reese asked again.

Ryan smiled, then laughed out loud. Both dogs turned to look at her curiously, but she waved them away as she trudged after them. Morgan had remembered the tabloid stories. In fact, she'd read her book. Reese, on the other hand, simply said, "I don't care who you are. I refuse to call you Catherine." Ryan didn't offer that her childhood nickname was Cat; she despised the name.

But that was that. Morgan had become her instant therapist, and Reese became the best buddy she never had before. For the first time in her life, she had friends. Not friends brought about by the Ryan-Barrett name but real friends. And they helped her heal. And she was finally writing again, something she'd been afraid to even attempt after all the scrutiny of her first novel. So yeah, that reclusive woman who lived on the mountain was becoming anything but a recluse. She was starting to open up again.

Except this winter. This winter she wanted to immerse herself in her writing. Nothing as deep as *Dancing on the Moon*. Written when she was ten years younger, it still had taken a lot out of her. No, the one she'd been toying with the last few months was much lighter. And as soon as Cooper's Peak dropped its load of snow—and after this latest storm, it could be any day now—she'd be stuck on the mountain until the spring thaw. Not that she wasn't already stuck. It was a three-hour hike through deep snow just to get to the lower part of the road. But once the avalanche ran, it would bury the forest road until spring. Last winter, she'd gone to the tropics, staying until her brother showed up. While they got along well enough, two weeks of his partying and never-ending string of women drove her back to the mountains. She stayed with Reese and Morgan until the roads were plowed high enough for her and the dogs to hike back up the mountain to her cabin. This year, though, she was writing. And being stuck up here for a few months, longer if she wanted to wait to get her Jeep out, was going to give her the time to finish the manuscript, she hoped. But after her first book, with the thrill of the Pulitzer Prize—and then the controversy afterward—she wasn't sure she wanted to publish it. Right now, just the fact that she was writing was enough. For now.

# CHAPTER TWO

"Great," Jen murmured. "Just great." She stopped the rented SUV, glancing out the windows in all directions, seeing nothing but snow, snow and more snow. Surely this wasn't the road to the lodge. She reached for the map, printed only as an afterthought. The directions seemed rather simple, and she thought even *she* couldn't get lost. Of course, not knowing where she was, the map was useless. "Writer's workshop. In February. In the mountains." Sure, sounded good on paper. She checked her phone again. Still no signal.

She got out, her boots sinking past her ankles into the fresh snow. She saw a road sign, its face covered in snow. She headed for it, then sunk nearly to her thighs; she was obviously off the road, the sign still five feet from her. She turned and struggled back to the SUV, then stomped her boots, knocking the snow off. Looking around, she realized she had only one option. And turning around wasn't it. She blew out a frosty breath, then got back inside, thankful she'd at least had the foresight to rent a four-wheel drive vehicle.

She drove on carefully, slowly, realizing too late that she had no idea where the road was. Minutes later, the front tires sunk like a rock.

"Oh no. *Seriously*?" She threw the car in reverse, only to have the rear tires spin uselessly.

\*\*\*

Ryan frowned as the sun reflected off of glass. She reached in the side pocket of her backpack and pulled out the compact binoculars she always carried.

"What the hell?" she murmured. A black SUV was buried up to the front bumper in snow. "What idiot tried to drive up here?"

The dogs whined beside her, ready to continue on with their hike. She reached down, petting them both absently, her eyes scanning the white landscape. She was torn. Someone could need help. But with the fresh snow from the other day, even using the snowshoes, it'd be a hard forty-five-minute hike to reach the SUV. Not to mention the forest road was right in the path of Cooper's Peak's avalanche chute. She'd been taking this route daily for the last week, hoping to witness the run, but she didn't want *that* close a view.

She figured they must have followed the snowmobile route up the mountain. Morgan had told her they'd closed the road in early January to vehicle traffic after they'd ceased plowing it. She scanned the area again, not seeing any movement. She was about to go on, assuming whoever was crazy enough to drive up the mountain in the first place had hiked back down on the same route, when a flash of blue caught her eye. She brought the binoculars up again, focusing well past the SUV.

"Hey," she yelled, waving her arms. "*Hey!* Get the hell out of there!" The person stopped, looking around for the sound of her voice. "Here," she yelled, waving her arms again. The idiot finally spotted her and waved back. Ryan lowered her binoculars with a shake of her head. "Damn tourist," she murmured. "Come on, girls."

The dogs ran ahead of her, and she hoped she wasn't putting all their lives in danger. She walked as fast as her snowshoes would allow, continuing to wave the person in her direction and away from the avalanche path. She glanced up the mountain, finding herself much too close to the edge of the chute. The mountain was swollen with snow and the warmer temperature today, coupled with the wind, made conditions ripe. It might have been her imagination, but she thought she felt a slight tremor under her feet; her heart thundered nervously in response.

"Come on," she yelled. "This way. Hurry!"

"I'm trying."

Ryan shook her head. *A woman. That figures.* She was close now. Fifty feet at least, but Ryan didn't want to chance going down the crest any further. She saw the woman struggling to walk in the snow, sinking each time above her knees. When she paused to rest, Ryan took another couple of steps in her direction.

"Come *on*," she said loudly.

The woman put her hands on her hips. "What's the rush?"

"You're in the goddamn path of an avalanche, that's the rush," she yelled back.

The woman's eyes widened, then, after a quick glance behind her, she hurried up the hill toward Ryan, using her hands to balance herself in the snow. Both dogs ran to meet her, barking their greeting. Ryan went down another few feet, holding out her hand to the woman. She took it, and Ryan nearly dragged her up the hill and over the crest.

"Walk in my tracks," she said quickly. "We've got to get the hell out of here."

All she heard was ragged breathing and the crunch of snow as she retraced her steps. She stopped suddenly, feeling a definite tremor, then another. "Oh fuck," she whispered. "Run! *Now!*"

The dogs seemed to know that danger was imminent as they both barked frantically, running back and forth toward Ryan, then away.

"I know, I know," she said. She was tempted to take off the snowshoes, but each second was precious. Her thighs burned as she concentrated on each step. Her shoes were caked with snow now, but she didn't pause to clean them. "Come on," she yelled behind her. "No time to waste."

"I can't," the woman cried. "My legs are cramping."

"Jesus," Ryan hissed. She turned, again grabbing the woman's hand and yanking her up. "Suck it up or we're both going to die," she said, her gaze meeting the woman's directly for the first time. She looked into eyes as blue as the mountain sky, eyes shrouded in fear. "Now come on."

The woman nodded, her gloved hand gripping tighter to Ryan's. They got no more than ten feet further when she heard a low rumble. She stopped, her glance going to the top of Cooper's Peak. She could literally see the mountain move. They were nearing a tree line, a scattering of spruce and firs dotting the landscape. She hoped the trees signaled that they were out of the path of the impending avalanche. Another two steps and she sunk past her thighs, her snowshoes scraping the side of a buried boulder. She pulled the woman past her, motioning to the spruce tree in front of them.

"Get behind it," she instructed, though she knew the tree would offer them little protection if the avalanche swept their way.

The whole mountain began to shake, the low rumble turning into an angry roar. Their hands were still gripped tightly together, but Ryan's eyes were glued to the show. The dogs whimpered beside her, and with her free hand she pulled them close to her. She watched in awe as the snow gave way, rushing down the chute at an amazing speed, covering everything in its path for hundreds of feet. A whoosh of cold air hit them as the snow sped past.

As quickly as it started, it was over. An eerie silence followed. She was aware of the absence of chattering jays and nutcrackers. Even the chickadees which constantly flitted among the trees were nowhere to be found.

"Wow."

Ryan turned, finding the woman's gaze still lingering on the mass of snow that now filled the crevice of the mountain, a space they had been scrambling out of only minutes earlier. A part of her was glad that there'd been someone here to share this moment with, someone other than the dogs. But the reality of the situation hit her. She pulled away from the woman, her eyebrows drawn together.

"Are you insane?"

The woman blinked several times as if considering the question literally. "Apparently." She moved from behind the tree, pausing to pet a dancing Sierra before wiping at the snow clinging to her pants. "It seemed like a good idea at the time."

"What? Crossing the barricade blocking the road? Driving on a closed road in the first place?"

The woman frowned. "What are you talking about? Aren't you from the lodge?"

It was Ryan's turn to frown. "The lodge? Patterson's Lodge?"

"Yes. I'm booked there for a workshop."

Ryan shook her head. *Unbelievable.* "Across the mountains there," she said, pointing, "you're about eight miles away. By car, you're about fifteen miles or so." She shrugged. "Or six or eight weeks, give or take."

"*What?*"

Ryan began the slow hike up the mountain, whistling for the dogs to follow. She heard the woman scrambling after her.

"Wait a minute. What do you mean, six or eight weeks?"

Ryan turned around, angry now. She pointed down to where the woman's car had been. Where it still was. Only now it was buried by a ton of snow. "What are you going to do? Drive out of here?" Ryan continued on. "You're stuck here," she tossed over her shoulder.

"Stuck?"

"Yeah, stuck. Stranded. Snowed in."

"Will you wait a minute? Please?"

*Jesus.* All Ryan could think about was that her plans for solitude had been shattered. Because some idiot woman got lost. So she stopped, waiting for the woman to catch up to her. Her anger faded, however, when she saw those sky-blue eyes filled with fear.

"I'm sorry, but where are we exactly? And...and who are you?"

It was only then that Ryan noticed the backpack slung over one shoulder and what appeared to be a laptop case strapped around her neck. She took the backpack from her, surprised at the heaviness of it. At least the woman had thought to get something from her car.

"That's Cooper's Peak," she said, motioning to the mountain behind them. "My cabin is on the next ridge. We're about fifteen miles south of Lake City. My name is... Ryan."

"I'm Jennifer Kincaid," she said. "Everyone calls me Jen." She tilted her head. "Ryan? Is that your last name?"

Ryan lifted a corner of her mouth quickly, then began walking. "It's just Ryan," she said.

# CHAPTER THREE

Jen stopped short, watching the inviting wisp of smoke circling above the cabin. She wasn't sure what she was expecting. Well, yes, she was. She was expecting a simple, weekend-type, one-room cabin. Nothing this elaborate.

Ryan turned back around, motioning to the door which was protected by a sharp, A-frame roof. Snow was piled around it four feet high.

"You coming in?"

Jen hesitated. "This is...this is where you live?"

"Uh-huh."

"Alone?"

"Well, with the girls," she said, glancing at the two dogs who waited patiently at the door.

Jen looked around, seeing nothing but white. Even the trees were still covered in glistening snow. "I don't see a road," she said.

"No." Ryan shrugged. "Well, there's the little Jeep road I use to get to the forest road, but that's covered with packed snow. Until at least May."

"So..." she said.

"So?"

"So what does that mean? May?" She could tell Ryan was quickly losing patience with her, but she didn't know this woman. She could be an ax murderer or something.

"May is when I can get my Jeep out and drive to the forest road. You know, the one you were on. The one that was closed. The one that had a barricade across it. So that *idiots* don't drive up here this time of year and get *stuck*. That's what I mean. So are you coming in or not? I'm cold and it's starting to snow again."

Okay, so the "idiot" word was meant for her. She took a deep breath and nodded. She didn't really have a choice. Darkness was nearly upon them. She looked up, watching the thickening snow falling around her. She mimicked Ryan, pausing to stomp her boots, knocking the snow off. The snowshoes Ryan had worn earlier were hanging on a hook beside the door, the poles shoved in a corner. Ryan silently handed her backpack to her, then closed the door behind them.

It was blissfully warm inside. Jen followed the dogs to the heat source—a black cast iron stove tucked into one corner. She dropped her backpack on the floor and tore her gloves off, holding out her hands to warm them. She hadn't realized how cold she was until she was inside.

Ryan joined her, pausing to remove her wool cap. Her dark hair was shaggy and unruly, but all she did was run her fingers through it a few times. Jen stared, just now noticing how attractive she was. Jen, too, took off her cap, knocking off clinging snow that fell to the stove with a sizzle.

Ryan watched her, her gaze sliding from the top of her head to her face. Jen followed with her hand, trying to put some semblance of order to her hair.

"I'm sorry," Ryan said. "I shouldn't have called you an idiot."

Jen smiled. "Well, I suppose it's the truth. I suck with maps, directions. I was just so sure I was on the right road."

"Technically, you were. During the summer, the forest road crosses the mountain and skirts Cooper's Peak. It's a nice shortcut for me when I go into town. But the lodge is not too far off of the highway, so you'd want to keep going up near Slumgullion Pass. On the *paved* road."

"So you...you do go into town then?"

Ryan simply raised her eyebrows.

"I mean, living out here like this, I assumed you were... like a...hermit," Jen said shyly.

Ryan gave a quick chuckle. "I prefer the term 'recluse.' Hermit sounds too much like an old crazy woman."

"Okay, but essentially the same thing," Jen said.

"And your point?"

Jen looked away from her dark gaze. "Just curious as to why," she said.

"I don't like people."

Jen took a step away from her. "I see," she said quietly.

Ryan held up her hands. "I'm harmless. Promise."

Jen eyed her suspiciously. "And I'm really stuck here?"

"Afraid so. Cooper's Peak drops its load every year. That's why they close the road."

"There was a metal bar across the road, yes. But tracks went around it and it looked well used," she explained. Of course, at the time, she should have paid more attention. She was just too focused on not getting lost.

"Snowmobilers use it since it's closed to vehicles," Ryan said. "But the avalanche buries the road—like it did your SUV—and they won't bother plowing the lower road until spring."

"Okay, I'm sorry, but all of that means what? Besides the fact that I'm an idiot," she said.

"Barring a helicopter rescue, that means you're stuck here until the lower road is cleared. You'll still have to hike down to that. Like I said, the road up here this high won't be clear until May. But I'd think by mid-April, the lower road will be passable."

*April?* "Two...two *months*?"

"Afraid so." Ryan moved away from the stove, motioning to the kitchen area. "Can I get you something to drink?"

"Actually, I really need to pee," Jen admitted, looking around and wondering if the cabin boasted modern facilities. The kitchen appeared to be fully functional.

"This way," Ryan said. Jen followed her down a short hallway with two doors. Ryan pushed open one, revealing a very large contemporary bathroom. Jen assumed the other was the bedroom. She closed the door behind her and leaned against it for a moment. The reality of her situation hit her full force, and she felt panic grip her. If Ryan hadn't come along, she would have most likely been caught in the avalanche and killed. And, if she'd survived it, then what? With temperatures well below freezing, she probably wouldn't have made it through the night.

But here she was, in a warm cabin about to use a flush toilet, in the middle of the proverbial nowhere. Miles from civilization. Sharing space with a "recluse." And two dogs. For six weeks. Possibly eight.

She met her reflection in the mirror, uncertainty and panic giving way to dread. Could she survive being stuck here for two months?

# CHAPTER FOUR

Ryan stood at the windows, staring out at the endless white landscape, the thick snow clouds ushering in dusk earlier than normal. *It could be worse*, she thought. She could have rescued a brash, obnoxious twenty-year-old male. Or a grandmother. So, yeah, it could be worse. Nevertheless, it did put a kink in her plans. She glanced at her desk, her eyes landing on her laptop. She supposed she could still get some writing done. Maybe Jennifer Kincaid would not be nosy and ask a lot of questions. She had her own laptop. Maybe she could stay entertained on her own. She turned when she heard the bathroom door open.

"Thank you."

She simply nodded and returned to her view. She felt Jen come up beside her.

"This is incredible. Did you build it?"

Ryan nodded. "Took two summers. It's not huge, but the workers could only work about five months each summer." She stepped back, deciding to give a quick litany of the cabin and get it over with.

"I have solar panels on the roof and a battery array to run the appliances and lights. I have propane to run the hot water heater, clothes dryer and stove." She motioned to the windows. "All of these oversized windows face south and west to optimize the natural light. As a rule, I don't turn on any lights until dusk. I have a couple of small wind turbines farther up the mountain. Nothing fancy but they help recharge the batteries. And I have a generator for those prolonged snowy days when the solar panels are useless." She went into the kitchen and turned on the faucet and quickly turned it off. "Running water. I have a well with a solar-powered pump. And I have a satellite dish for both TV and Internet." She shrugged. "All the comforts of home."

Jen smiled. "Some hermit you are," she said teasingly. "So that means we have e-mail?"

"Yes, but not at the moment. After a snowstorm, the dish is covered. It takes a day or two for the snow on it to melt," she explained. "Same with the solar panels. I have steps built to the roof so I can get up there and sweep them off. The dish, though, is on a tower, so I can't get to it."

Jen nodded. "I just need to let someone know I'm okay. I assume—when I don't show up at the lodge—that they'll call my agent or someone."

"Your agent?"

"Yes. It was a writer's workshop."

Ryan stared at her. *She's a writer?* Yeah, it just got worse.

***

"So, a writer, huh? Published?"

Jen nodded and took the cup of coffee Ryan offered. "Thanks. And yes, published. I write self-help books," she said. "Well, three so far. I know I'm not a literary genius, but I really want to write a novel." She smiled shyly. "Who doesn't, right? I have an idea for one, I just don't quite know how to go about it. That's why I signed up for the workshop. One month of intense hands-on instruction."

"At the Pattersons' lodge?" Ryan asked doubtfully. She couldn't imagine who would be up here teaching such a class. In February, no less.

"Yes. It's sponsored by the Colorado Writers Group. They have quite a lineup of talented instructors." Jen sipped from her coffee, her glance meeting Ryan's above the cup. "One month. Fiction only. They teach various formats, structures and techniques. Character development and dialogue." She wrinkled up her nose. "I suck with dialogue."

"So you've tried to write before?"

"Yes. *Tried* being the key word there. Like I said, I've only written self-help books."

Ryan's instinct told her to steer the conversation elsewhere, but she was curious. Jennifer Kincaid was nearly bubbling with enthusiasm. Something she herself once had.

"So how does one write a self-help book?"

"Research, research, research. Especially if you don't have *initials* after your name."

"Like PhD or MD?"

"Exactly." Jen reached for the sugar bowl and added a small amount to her coffee. "But really, I got the idea after reading one of Sara Michaels' books." She looked up. "Do you know who she is? She's from Denver."

Ryan shook her head. "No."

"Do you remember several years ago, Senator Michaels was running for president? He went psycho and tried to have his daughter killed. Remember?"

"Oh, yeah. The lesbian daughter," Ryan said. "She was hiking with a group of women over in the Collegiate Peaks area."

"Yes, that's the one. Her work evolved into a center in Denver where people—mostly women—go for classes on how to better themselves. She's quite popular. Anyway, I read a couple of her books." She shrugged. "Really, all self-help books are pretty much the same. So I thought, why can't I write one?"

Ryan kept her smile hidden, surprised at how forthright Jen was being. "So you stole her ideas?"

Jen laughed. "Not exactly. My books tend to lean toward meditation and inner peace to help cope with life's daily issues. You know—work, finances, spouse, kids. It targets women, obviously. My message is to take time for yourself," she said. "And use meditation—and yoga—to tap into that magical energy we all have inside. I encourage people to take at least one hour each day that does not involve work or home or spouse or kids. One hour just for you." Jen's grin was infectious. "Doesn't that sound wonderful?"

Ryan arched an eyebrow skeptically. "And you wrote a book about that?"

"Yes. Amazing, isn't it?"

"And people bought it?"

"Yes. Self-help books are all the rage."

"And so you're an expert on meditation and stuff?"

Jen brushed the bangs off of her forehead and sighed. "Okay, while my intentions were good, I will concede that no, I'm not an expert. Who is? I mean, I've taken my share of yoga classes. I've read countless books on meditation and the benefits of tapping into your own resources, your own energy. I do know what I'm talking about," she said almost defensively.

"So, just regurgitated information?"

"Isn't everything? You're just rewording it, calling it something different. I mean, look at all of the popular diets. Low carb this and low carb that. All the same, yet you can buy ten or twelve different books. All they've done is just tweak a few things. My books are no different."

"So you're saying that anyone could write a self-help book?"

"Exactly."

"But if it doesn't work, don't you lose credibility?"

"That's the secret. Whether it works or not is up to the reader. As the author, all I promise is that 'if you follow the instructions completely' then it'll work."

"I see. And as the author, you make it virtually impossible for anyone to follow it *completely* so you're off the hook." Jen smiled again, and Ryan found she was not immune to her enthusiasm...or her good looks. She was absolutely adorable.

"See? You too could write one. The readers who follow it almost to the T, they get results. How could they not? But if they don't get what was promised, they put the blame on themselves. Because they didn't follow it one hundred percent. And quite frankly, most will start out like gangbusters, only to let real life get in the way. So the failure, again, is their own."

"Sounds simple."

"It is. Like I said, anyone can write one. But not just anyone can write a real novel. Thus, the writer's workshop." They were quiet, both sipping their coffee. Then Jen pushed her cup away and folded her hands together. "What about this helicopter rescue you mentioned?"

Ryan shrugged. "Up this high, they'd have to wait for optimal wind conditions. But since it's not a medical emergency, I'm not sure what kind of priority you'd have. It would be fairly expensive too."

"I see. So, I'm really stuck then."

"You're really stuck."

"But you are *intentionally* stuck. Right? I mean, you said your Jeep road was covered with snow until May."

"Well, like I said, I'm—"

"A recluse. Right," Jen said. "So what's your story?"

Ryan froze, not able to meet her eyes. After spending nearly ten years hiding from the public, only now was she beginning to feel almost normal. Well, as normal as living a solitary life can be. She had no wish to relive the humiliation of the controversy that broke out after the Pulitzer. But instead of telling Jen to mind her own business, she feigned indifference.

"No story."

"There has to be a story. You're living up here, isolated. Intentionally, it seems. I mean, letting yourself get snowed in and all."

Ryan tapped her fingers against her cup, trying to appear disinterested. "I told you, I don't like people."

Jen smiled. "You forget. I've researched all this crap to death. *I just don't like people* is not a reason for all this," she said, waving her hands at the cabin. "Hermits—or a recluse, as you prefer—want to remove themselves from society. They just want to disappear."

"Yeah? And?"

"If that was truly the case, you wouldn't have a satellite dish for TV. And you wouldn't bother with Internet."

"I don't necessarily want to forget about the world, I just want it to forget about me."

Jen shrugged. "You made mention that you go into town and you knew the lodge by name. That tells me that you're not quite as reclusive as you pretend."

Ryan stared at her, knowing she had no retort to her claim. She looked away, saying nothing. If this was going to be a prelude to the kinds of conversations they were going to have for the next few weeks, she might very well fling herself into the canyon. So she stood, her glance going to the dogs, both sleeping near the stove.

"I should start dinner," she said abruptly.

"Oh, I didn't even think about that," Jen said. "I promise, I don't eat much."

"I have plenty. The pantries are stocked. Six weeks, even eight, isn't all that long, you know."

"Speak for yourself," Jen said with a laugh.

"We should have Internet back in a day or so. Hopefully that will keep you occupied."

"What about you? What do you do to keep occupied?"

Ryan couldn't help to take a quick, longing peek at her laptop. She needed to write. She would go stark raving mad if she didn't. She was just getting a good feel for the story and she had words bouncing around in her head, begging to get out. But that wasn't something she could announce. "I have plenty of chores to keep me busy," she said instead.

To her chagrin, Jen followed her into the kitchen, pulling out one of the two barstools. Ryan felt self-conscious as she stared into the pantry, trying to decide on dinner. Despite her words, eight weeks was going to be an eternity.

"I can help with some of your chores, you know. Like cooking," Jen offered. "And I mean, don't go to any trouble on my account."

Ryan glanced at her, then back to the pantry, eyeing the soup cans.

"You don't talk much, do you?"

Ryan bit her lower lip. God, she had to have rescued a chatterbox, didn't she? She sighed, grabbing a couple of cans of soup and holding them up for her guest to inspect. "Hermit and all, not used to talking," she offered as way of an excuse.

"Oh, of course. I'm sorry. I tend to talk a lot, especially when I'm nervous."

Ryan pulled out a pot. "Are you nervous?"

"Well, yeah," Jen said with a short laugh. "I mean, I'm apparently stuck here. You're a stranger to me. I don't know you, yet I'm at your mercy, basically. And who's to say you don't make a habit of abducting unsuspecting tourists and then hacking their bodies into little pieces and burying them in your snow-covered backyard?"

Jen had a smile on her face, but there was a wariness in her eyes that Ryan found surprising. Was she really afraid of her? And here Ryan thought she was being on her best behavior.

"You know, maybe you should be a novelist," she said with a slight smile. "Your imagination is certainly active."

# CHAPTER FIVE

Sleeping arrangements had not occurred to her. She had spent the evening trying to curb her curiosity and limit her questions, even though Ryan rarely answered one anyway. Dinner had been simple. Canned soup. She hadn't had much of an appetite so the light fare was perfect. She'd sorted through the backpack she'd had the forethought to grab from the SUV. It contained two pairs of jeans, three long-sleeved T-shirts, two bulky sweaters, and thankfully, panties and bras. Not much for several weeks but Ryan assured her the utility room contained a functioning washer and dryer. She'd left the backpack on the floor, not wanting to get into Ryan's space. Ryan had watched her doing inventory of the pack but had not commented, other than to mention laundry. The silence continued after their quick dinner. The sitting area contained one recliner, which Ryan used, and a small, undersized sofa, which Jen had claimed. The dogs took the rug. The stove kept the area plenty warm and Jen would admit that it was cozy. The only light came from a lamp positioned between them and the stove, which gave off a cheery glow, making for a comfortable end to the day. Quiet, but comfortable. They'd both had their laptops out, Ryan tapping away on something she chose not to talk about and Jen deciding to write a journal about her adventure so far. Not exactly a writer's workshop but in case something happened to her—like getting hacked up into tiny pieces—maybe someone would find her journal and know of her fate. But at ten minutes before ten, Ryan had closed her laptop and stood, pausing to stretch. She said nothing as she slipped on her coat and took the dogs outside, presumably for a potty break. Jen took this as a sign of bedtime.

Now, after her turn in the bathroom—using a donated toothbrush from Ryan—she waited for instructions. Ryan and the dogs were in the bedroom and Jen stood nervously in the small hallway.

"You coming or what?"

The kitchen and sitting areas were dark. She turned toward the bedroom, finding Ryan standing by the bed, a lit lamp on either side. Jen looked at her and swallowed.

"You're offering to share your bed?" she asked quietly.

"Do you have another idea?"

"I can probably fit on the sofa," Jen suggested.

"Yeah, you're pretty short. You'd probably fit. Although if you have to spend six or eight weeks on it, that's going to get very old."

Jen drew her brows together. "Short? I'm not short."

Ryan said nothing as she pulled back the covers. Then, as if an afterthought, "The stove in here should last until morning. But if you get up to pee, toss a log inside, would you?"

Ryan turned out the lamp on her side and got in the bed, leaving Jen standing in the doorway. She sighed. *Had to get lost, didn't you?* Speaking of getting old, being stuck here with a woman who barely speaks could get very tiresome. Could be worse though, she thought. She could have been buried in an avalanche. But still, she hesitated. She'd shared a bed with only one other person in her entire life. And even then, she wasn't comfortable. Brad was used to it now and it was rare that he stayed the night anymore.

She let out a deep breath again, taking one last look into the darkened living room, seeing a faint glow through the window. The moon? Maybe tomorrow would prove sunny. Ryan had mentioned a hike up along the ridge to see if they could get a signal on her phone. Jen assumed when she didn't show up at the lodge that someone would call her agent as she was the one who had booked her into the workshop. She needed to let Susan know she was okay, at least. And Brad, of course.

She maneuvered around the dogs that were sprawled out on the rug. Neither lifted their heads, but their eyes followed her progress as she went to the opposite side of the bed. Ryan had her back to her and Jen quietly lifted the covers, then realized she was still completely dressed. She kicked off her boots and stepped out of her jeans, leaving her socks on. She debated on whether to remove her sweater as well and decided to leave it on. She turned the light out, then eased into bed, hugging the side, staying as far away from Ryan as possible. On her back, she stared at the ceiling, her eyes adjusting to the darkness, broken only by the orange glow that escaped the confines of the stove, their heat source for the night. She should be exhausted after the stressful day she'd had, yet she felt wide awake. The minutes ticked away slowly as her gaze remained fixed on the ceiling. Sleep would not come. Even so, Ryan's voice startled her.

"If you're worried, I promise I won't chop you into little pieces and bury you in the snow."

"That's comforting. Thanks." Jen wondered how Ryan knew she wasn't asleep. She hadn't moved a muscle since she'd gotten in the bed.

"I couldn't bury you in the snow anyway. You know it's going to melt eventually. There'd be evidence."

Jen's eyes widened and she swallowed nervously. After what seemed an abnormally long moment of silence, Ryan rolled over onto her back.

"I could, I suppose, haul you up to the edge of Cooper's Peak and drop you into Cutter's Canyon. Old Johnnie Cutter would be the only one who might possibly stumble on your body someday."

Jen could barely breathe, and she was afraid to move a muscle. *She really is a crazy old hermit.* Panic set in and she was about to bolt from the bed when Ryan clamped a hand around her arm. Jen just barely stifled a scream.

"I'm *kidding*," Ryan said, a smile in her voice. "You know that, right?"

Jen took a deep breath, swallowing down her fear. "So are you telling me you have a sense of humor? I mean, it's a sick one, but still..."

Ryan gave a short laugh, then again rolled over away from her. "Goodnight, Jennifer Kincaid."

Jen turned her head slowly, staring at the back of Ryan's head. "Goodnight." Despite feeling less threatened, she knew she'd still have a hard time falling asleep. Growing up the way she had, with the fear of *everything* instilled in her, having someone in her bed was an abnormality.

Even after all these years with Brad, she still couldn't sleep comfortably with him. It was on a rare occasion that he suggested he stay the night. Or vice versa. Now, surprisingly, she found herself drifting off. She let her eyes slip closed, giving in to her exhaustion.

# CHAPTER SIX

The sun was magnificently bright, and Ryan shielded her eyes, turning to find Jen staring off across the mountains, her cheeks red from the wind but a slight smile on her face. *God, she's pretty.* Jen glanced at Ryan, as if sensing her watching.

"It's so beautiful. Simple words can't do it justice."

Ryan nodded. "I can think of lots of words in a dictionary where this scene could be used as the definition. Like 'pristine.'"

Jen looked back toward the cabin, the trees white and laden with snow. She glanced at Ryan. "Immaculate."

Ryan nodded. "Exhilarating."

Jen tilted her head, a smile on her face. "Inspirational."

"Splendor."

"Radiance."

Ryan laughed. "Okay. So you get the idea." She walked on, hearing Jen following. Sierra and Kia were running ahead of them, and Ryan followed their tracks. They had a trail established, keeping the snow packed down. Not only was the ridge the only place she could get a cell signal, it was also the spot for a perfect sunset. "So, Santa Fe, huh?"

"Yes."

"Rented the SUV, drove from Santa Fe, through the mountains, up Wolf Creek Pass, through Creede to Lake City. In the dead of winter. For a writer's retreat?"

"That's the point. It's the dead of winter. You're stuck in a lodge. You don't lose your focus. You want to get snowed in."

"Well, you got that part right, at least."

"Are you going to call me an idiot again?"

"No, no. I think we're past that."

Jen huffed behind her, her feet crunching loudly in the snow. "Like I said, I suck with directions. Always have," she explained. "But this seemed so straightforward."

Ryan stopped, letting Jen catch her breath. Both dogs came running back down toward them, their tongues hanging out as they danced in the snow. Ryan petted each of them, then watched as Jen did the same.

"So who's going to miss you?"

Jen looked up, frowning. "What?"

"You know, when you don't show at the lodge. Who are they going to call? Boyfriend? Husband?"

Jen shook her head. "No. They'll call Susan, my agent. Brad wasn't all that enthused about me taking this trip. He and Susan don't really get along, but I suppose she'll call him."

"Brad?"

"Boyfriend," Jen said. Then she shrugged. "I guess. I mean, he wants to get married."

"Fiancé then?"

Jen looked past her, to the west where the towering peaks of the San Juan Mountains hovered. She had a pensive look on her face. Ryan wondered what thoughts were going through her mind. She turned back to Ryan, and again Ryan was stunned by the blueness of her eyes.

"He hasn't officially asked. And there's no ring," she said, holding up her gloved hands.

Ryan moved on, continuing up the trail. "So you're not ready?"

Jen laughed. "That's so cliché, isn't it?"

"Well, it's an excuse, anyway."

"Yes. And I shouldn't need an excuse."

Ryan stopped again. "So?"

But Jen waved her on. "No. I don't want to talk about it. Besides, last night you gave me the impression that you don't like to talk. Why all the questions today?"

What could she say? The curiosity was brought about by the writer in her. Of course, it wouldn't do to tell Jen that. She could only imagine her reaction to that bit of news. "Just making conversation," she said instead.

Up this high along the ridge, trees were few and far between, only a handful of hearty firs taking hold in the rocks. A group of noisy nutcrackers gathered in one, shaking the snow from the branches as they landed.

"What are they?" Jen asked.

"Clark's nutcrackers," she said. "I've got some birdseed at the cabin. I'm just not real diligent about keeping the feeders filled. We can put some out later, if you like."

Their eyes met for a brief moment, and Jen nodded. "I'd like that."

Ryan walked a few more feet, taking out her cell phone. She checked the signal. Only three bars, but enough for a call. "Got a signal."

"Do you know the number to the lodge?"

"No. I'll just call Chief Daniels," she said, finding Reese's number in her contact list.

"Who is that?"

"Sheriff," she explained. "And a friend."

Jen laughed. "A friend? Do hermits have friends?"

"I'm allowed two," Ryan said with a smile, turning away from Jen as Reese answered.

"Hey, Ryan. What a surprise. Everything okay up there?"

"Yeah. I guess," she said, glancing at Jen. "Cooper's Peak dropped its load," she said.

"I figured. So did Cutter's Chute," Reese said. "You got your wish. You're stuck up there now. How's the writing going?"

"At a standstill," she said. "I kinda have company," she said quietly, although Jen did not appear to be listening. She was playing with the dogs, tossing snowballs up in the air and laughing delightfully as the dogs attempted to catch them. "Jennifer Kincaid," she said. "She was on her way to Patterson's Lodge when she got stranded."

"What the hell was she doing up there?"

"She thought she would take the forest road across the mountain."

"In the *winter*? That road's been closed for two months."

"Yeah. We've been over all that already," Ryan said. "Avalanche buried her vehicle."

"She's damn lucky. Do I need to request a helicopter rescue?"

Ryan glanced over at Jen who still seemed oblivious to the conversation. Six weeks? Maybe eight? It could all be over within a few days if the winds died down. Of course, they would charge Jen a fortune for the rescue. She stared at her, her cheeks red and glowing, her smile lighting up her face as she played with the dogs. *Beautiful.* "No," she said, surprising herself with the answer. "No need for a rescue mission. We'll wait until they plow the lower road, then hike down."

"That's gonna be at least another six weeks yet," Reese cautioned.

"Yeah. I know. But I have enough supplies for both of us."

"Damn. What's wrong with you? Let me guess. She's young and pretty?"

Ryan laughed, again looking over at Jen. This time, Jen was looking back at her. "Definitely. Once I get satellite back, I'll shoot you guys an e-mail and let you know what happened and let you get in touch with her rental agency. In the meantime, can you call Ellen? She's got her contact information."

"Will do. I'll take care of it. Keep in touch when you can."

"Yeah. I'll check in occasionally."

"Do that. I know Morgan is going to be pestering me for information. You might send a picture of this woman, huh?"

Ryan smiled and nodded. "I'll see what I can do."

She disconnected, then held the phone out to Jen. "You want to call someone? Brad?"

Jen shook her head. "My phone was in the SUV," she said. "Like most people, I don't memorize numbers anymore."

"Okay. Well, Reese said she'd call Ellen, the owner of the lodge."

Jen studied her silently for a moment. "So you're friends with the sheriff?"

"Yes."

"Did you...get into trouble or something?"

Ryan laughed. "Yeah. I tried to hack up a tourist last summer." She whistled for the dogs, and they both came running. "I met Reese and Morgan—that's her partner—at Sloan's Bar in Lake City. Real hermits aren't supposed to go into town for burgers."

"So they've revoked your membership?"

"Yeah," she said, heading back down toward the cabin. "We became friends. Lesbians do tend to stick together." Several steps later, she realized Jen was no longer following her. She turned back around, finding Jen stopped, staring at her. "What?"

"You're...you're a...*lesbian*?"

Ryan shrugged. "You didn't know?"

"How would I know? You didn't mention it. And you're not wearing a sign."

"Sorry. I just assumed." She continued on, shaking her head. *Great, now you've scared the poor girl.* Maybe she should reconsider the helicopter rescue.

"We...we slept in the same bed."

Ryan laughed. "Yeah, but lucky for you, I'm not contagious."

"But—"

Ryan stopped again. "What is it? Are you afraid of me now? You think maybe I'll try something and if you don't give in to my advances, I'll actually hack you up into little pieces?" She smiled but knew it didn't reach her eyes. "Trust me, straight women with fiancés waiting in the wings don't excite me in the least. You're perfectly safe."

"It's just...you're nothing like what my grandfather used to preach about."

"Huh?"

# CHAPTER SEVEN

Jen tried not to stare, but she couldn't help it. Ryan was so attractive. Nothing like the women her grandfather described as being homosexual. She wasn't wearing men's clothing. Well, no more than she herself was, she thought as she glanced at her jeans and boots. Ryan wasn't pretending to be a man, like her grandfather said they did. She looked *normal*. And as sheltered a life as Jen had had, in the last seven or eight years she'd been exposed to a lot. It wasn't as if she'd been living under a rock. And she was a fan of Sara Michaels' work and she too was normal. But still...

"You're staring," Ryan said without looking up from her laptop.

"I'm sorry."

Jen quickly turned her attention to her journal, her fingers lightly tapping the keys at random, no words coming to her. Ryan, on the other hand, seemed to be writing furiously, her fingers flying across the keys in a graceful motion. They stilled, and Jen realized she was staring again.

"Look, it's not like I'm an alien or anything," Ryan said. "Just a woman, nothing more, nothing less."

"I'm sorry," Jen said again.

Ryan let out a heavy breath. "You have questions. Ask."

"My grandfather said...well, never mind."

"Yeah, what's with your grandfather?"

Jen bit her lip. "He was a preacher. A minister," she said. "He and my grandmother raised me."

Ryan's smile was humorless. "Great," she said dryly. "I've rescued a homophobe."

"He died," Jen blurted out. "Last year."

"And?"

Jen took a deep breath, wondering why she felt the need to explain. "I was *extremely* sheltered. My mother was fifteen when I was born. She was the epitome of the wild preacher's daughter," she said. "Drugs, alcohol...and sex."

"So they raised you?"

"Yes. And every transgression and sin that my mother committed, I paid for. I was homeschooled," she said. "I had no friends to speak of. And I was socially inept." She glanced at Ryan. "Still am in some respects."

"I see. So you're not a homophobe then?"

"No. I don't think so. I just don't have any gay friends. Not that I'm insinuating you and I are friends," she added quickly. "I was just...surprised, I guess. Socially inept and all," she said with a smile.

"Well, they must have done something right," Ryan said. "You've written three books."

Jen laughed. "Self-*help* books," she corrected. "Something I kept a secret from them, by the way. They wouldn't approve." She leaned back, staring at the ceiling, picturing her grandfather's face. Oh, she could only imagine his scorn. "I grew up in West Texas, near Lubbock," she said.

"That explains the accent then," Ryan said.

"I don't have an accent," she insisted. "I worked very hard to lose it."

"Okay, you don't have an accent," Ryan said, appeasing her.

Jen grinned at her, then looked away. "My mother got arrested when she was nineteen. That's when my grandparents got legal custody of me. My mother wasn't around much after that. I'd see her a couple of times a year when she'd come around for money." Jen glanced at her again, seeing that she had Ryan's full attention. "Because she was so bad, they were extra strict with me. I mean, I couldn't do *anything*. But since I didn't have any friends, there weren't a lot of options anyway."

"Homeschooled all the way through?"

"Yes." Jen laughed. "If they could have figured out a way, I'm certain they would have homeschooled me for my college degree as well. But it was nearly that bad. They would not hear of me staying in the dorms. They allowed me to go all the way to Lubbock—forty miles away—to college," she said sarcastically, "and to stay with a friend of theirs. A widow. A very bitter woman who never smiled. Her entire life revolved around the church. Therefore, so did mine. And every Friday after class, I had to drive home to my grandparents' house. I wasn't allowed to return to Lubbock until Sunday afternoon."

"Resentful?"

Was that the word she would use? She nodded. "Yes. Resentful. Once I moved to Santa Fe, I separated myself from them more and more."

"You missed out on a lot growing up."

"I know." Jen sighed. "I didn't know it at the time, of course. Back then, there was never a question of me going against their wishes."

"So you didn't go through a rebellious stage?"

"I was afraid to. Even in college, I had very few friends. I met Brad there. He was a journalism major, so we had several classes together. He became my first real friend."

"And lover?"

Jen blushed. "We started dating when I was a senior, and even then, I had to keep that a secret from them. He wasn't from the church, you know," she said mockingly.

"Your mother was never in the picture?"

"Not when I was younger, no. She's married now. Lives in Dallas. They have two children. To her credit, she tried to get me to live with her, but my grandparents wouldn't hear of it. We're closer now, but still, our relationship was already damaged. Actually, my relationship with my grandmother is strained as well. I don't talk to her very often."

"So how did you escape to Santa Fe?"

"After college, I got a job at Anasazi Press. Brad is from Santa Fe originally," she explained. "They threw a fit about me moving there, but they couldn't very well make me move back home with them, even though they strongly suggested it. It was my first act of defiance. Besides, Lubbock offered nothing for me."

"And they still didn't know Brad was in the picture?"

"No. Ironically, Anasazi Press had published the first self-help book that I ever read." She laughed. "I'm certain I'm one of the few people who read it. *Party Girl! How to Shake the Wallflower Image.*" She rolled her eyes. "It was way over the top. Especially for me. But it did open my eyes about a few things. I gradually broke out of my shell, but I never reached that party girl stage."

"You're so attractive, I can't imagine 'wallflower' applying to you," Ryan said. "You must have had guys hanging around."

"Thank you. But I didn't dress to call attention to myself. And I wore old-fashioned glasses, nothing stylish. Not so attractive. And anyway, as soon as guys found out I wasn't going to sleep with them, they left. By my senior year, I was pretty much over my shyness. I had a few close friends, and I had Brad."

"So he's your one and only boyfriend?"

Jen looked away from Ryan's curious stare. "Yes. I dated a preacher's son a couple of times, but all he was interested in was seeing if he could get past second base."

Ryan laughed. "And did he?"

Jen blushed again, wondering why she was telling Ryan this. "I let him touch my breasts—through my shirt—and even then I thought I'd burn in hell."

Ryan looked at her thoughtfully. "I can't relate. Certainly not to a boy touching my breasts and not even the burning in hell part. Religion was never a part of my life."

Jen watched her expression change. The openness she'd shared in that brief moment was gone, and a mask was in its place. Jen was just barely able to stifle her curiosity. That was the first bit of personal information Ryan had divulged.

The silence continued, with Ryan tapping away on her laptop and Jen adding to the journal she'd started. Although it was sunny outside, the wind had picked up, making the windows rattle around them. The stove burned hotly, keeping the inside of the cabin warm enough for Jen to lose her sweater. Ryan was in her recliner, her legs stretched out, her jeans replaced by comfortable-looking sweatpants.

"Would you like a pair?"

Jen realized she'd been staring again, and she smiled. "Can you spare some? Although, as you mentioned last night, I am a little shorter than you are."

Ryan closed her laptop and went in the direction of the bedroom. Jen blew out a long breath, turning to glance back out the windows. Ryan was nice enough. Pleasant, in fact. Sometimes. But other times, like now, she was withdrawn. Silent. Dare she say brooding? Or was she just moody?

Jen couldn't blame her. Whether she called her a recluse or not, Ryan obviously wanted to be alone. Having someone thrown in your lap unexpectedly—and for possibly eight weeks—would no doubt put anyone in a foul mood.

"Here you go," Ryan said, tossing the sweats at her. "My shortest pair."

"Thanks."

# CHAPTER EIGHT

Ryan scooped rice onto a plate, then added a generous amount of the chicken mixture on top. It was a dish Morgan had taught her—salsa chicken. Ryan had stopped by unexpectedly one evening, and Morgan had thrown together this: small pieces of chicken breasts sautéed with celery, carrots, onions, a can of stewed tomatoes and salsa. It was easy and quick, and Ryan had added it to her list of favorites. But her supply of fresh foods was dwindling, and she'd just barely salvaged the last of the celery for this dish. She still had onions and potatoes. Other than that, they would have to rely on canned foods for the rest of the winter.

She felt Jen watching her, but she didn't look up. Jen was full of questions, none of which Ryan was prepared to answer. It would be best if Jen remained just a little afraid of her. Perhaps it would limit her inquisitiveness.

"Are you going to avoid talking to me the whole time I'm here?"

Ryan glanced up, raising her eyebrows questioningly.

"I know you want to remain this mysterious recluse," Jen said, "but I think I have a right to know *something* about you. I am putting my welfare in your hands, after all."

Ryan smiled at this. "Yes, you did drive up a closed mountain road during an impending avalanche, didn't you? You didn't so much 'put' your welfare into my hands, though, as thrust it there. It's not like you had any other choices. Or that I did, for that matter."

"So you're going to clam up anytime we talk about personal things? Are you, like, wanted by the law or something?"

"Seeing as how I called the county sheriff on your behalf, I hardly think so," she said with a smirk.

"Then why won't you talk to me?"

"I told you, I don't like people. I don't like questions. I choose to live up here alone so that I can avoid both of those," she said sharply, hoping to end the conversation.

Jen pulled out a barstool and sat down, accepting the plate that Ryan slid her way. Ryan walked around the bar and sat next to her, thinking it would be rude to eat her dinner in the recliner the way she usually did.

"This is good," Jen said. "Thank you. I know you didn't expect to have to feed someone else."

Ryan shrugged. "I have to cook anyway. It's no problem." She could feel Jen studying her, could sense questions forming in her mind. She could always just tell her who she really was, but she could only imagine the hundreds of additional questions that would bring.

"What are you running from?"

Ryan glanced at her, knowing she was fishing. "Nothing."

"I write self-help books. And while I'm not an expert on anything, I've researched behaviors to death. And you, the mysterious Ryan, are running—hiding—from something."

"Is that what you think?" God, she wished Jen would just let it rest.

"A lot of people don't like other people, but they don't choose to live somewhere where they are literally cut off from the outside world. Not unless they are hiding from that outside world."

"Perhaps I have a mental disorder," Ryan said. "That should cause you some concern."

Jen put her fork down, taking a drink from her water glass instead. "You're trying to scare me."

"Am I? Will that do it?" Ryan looked at her. "I thought you were already scared. You know, having to sleep in the same bed as a lesbian."

Jen smiled. "Yes, that was a shock. But you don't seem all that threatening." She leaned closer and bumped her arm playfully. "Are you medicated?"

Ryan laughed. "No. I have no mental disorder. At least I don't think so." She relaxed, knowing she couldn't keep up this façade of pretending not to like her indefinitely. It could be so much worse. She decided to throw her a bone, a bit of information about her life. Maybe she'd be sensitive enough to leave it at that.

"My family is...wealthy," she said. "And we don't see eye-to-eye."

"Because you're...gay?"

"No. The reason why doesn't matter. But it afforded me the opportunity to buy this land, build this cabin." She paused. "My solitude is for my own sanity."

"Okay. Then what do you do?"

"Do?"

"Yeah. You must do something to keep sane. Laptop?"

"What about it?" she asked cautiously.

"You keep busy with something," Jen said, her voice slightly accusing.

Ryan wondered if Jen could see the possible lies and excuses that popped into her mind as she tried to find something appropriate to say. There were dozens of them, and what she blurted out was probably the worst possible choice. She cringed as she heard the words leave her mouth.

"I'm...an editor."

Jen's interest was obviously piqued. "An editor? Like in publishing?"

Ryan nodded, desperately trying to think of a graceful way out of this.

"So when I told you I'd written several self-help books, you didn't think to mention this then? I mean, we have something in common, at least." Jen looked at her accusingly. "Which publisher do you work for?"

Ryan shoved a forkful of her dinner into her mouth, stalling. "I freelance," she mumbled.

"Freelance?"

Ryan nodded, not elaborating.

Jen put her elbows on the bar, watching her. "So you have a project now?"

Ryan nodded again. "Yes."

Jen picked up her fork again. "You're doing an awful lot of typing. What are you doing? Rewriting the whole manuscript?"

"First-time writer. I'm making a lot of notes." She stood, scooting the barstool away and taking her half-eaten dinner to the sink, effectively ending the conversation. *An editor? Yeah, way to think on your feet,* she chastised herself.

She felt Jen watching her as she slipped on her coat and gloves. She avoided looking at her. "Girls." Both dogs jumped to attention, Sierra beating Kia to the door, as was the norm. They burst out into the darkness, the air bitterly cold after the warmth of the cabin. The snow crunched beneath her boots, and her breath frosted around her. The moon was only a sliver, but the light was enough, reflecting off of the snow, to allow her to move about without a flashlight. The dogs ran up the trail ahead of her. They knew the nighttime routine. She would wait close to the cabin as they did their business. They would return a few minutes later, snow clinging to their fur, tongues hanging out regardless of the temperature. They would stare at her, waiting on her to let them back inside the warm cabin.

She looked skyward, where a million stars were twinkling. She loved nights like this. Silent, dark and windless. So quiet, in fact, she could hear each breath she took, hear each steady beat of her heart. It was almost a form of meditation, for she could hold no thoughts in her mind as it emptied itself of contemplation and filled itself with a relaxing nothingness.

Tonight, however, her mind remained fixed on the uninvited guest who was sharing her cabin. An inquisitive guest, no less. Ryan's wish to remain anonymous was on shaky ground. She wouldn't tell her the truth. *Catherine Ryan-Barrett.* No, Jen would want to know about her family and the hotel and casino business. And then about the Pulitzer Prize and if she'd *really* been the one to write the book. Or whether as the tabloids said—and as her parents had believed despite her protests to the contrary—there had been a ghostwriter. She bit her lip, remembering how betrayed she'd felt at the time.

No, Ryan had no desire to answer any of the hundreds of questions Jen would ask if she knew who she was. The better option, should Jen ask again, would be to tell her she was trying her own hand at writing, chronicling her adventures of living alone up here on the mountain, in winter. Maybe that would appease her.

Ryan smiled quickly and shook her head. More likely, it would lead her to want to read what she was writing, to *discuss* it. No, she'd probably be better off sticking with the editor story, half-assed as it was.

# CHAPTER NINE

Jen stood at the window staring out, the bright sunshine a contradiction to the subzero temperatures that had settled over the cabin. It was her sixth day of being stranded, but she no longer thought of it that way. She would go stark, raving mad if she continued to think of it as a jail sentence, marking off each day one by one. Which was how she'd gotten through the first three. But Ryan's sullen moods gradually had disappeared, and Jen now only occasionally found a brooding look on her face, mostly when Ryan thought she wasn't watching.

Their evenings had taken on a routine, usually with both of them cradling laptops. She was beyond curious as to what Ryan was working on, but so far she'd been able to curtail any questions. She knew Ryan hated personal questions. But that didn't mean she couldn't ask professional ones. Since Ryan was an editor and since Jen was supposed to be at a writer's workshop, she'd instead peppered Ryan with questions about technical matters and about wordsmithing. At first, her answers were short and to the point. Then Ryan had suggested she do an exercise. She gave her a subject—a girl from a poverty-stricken family was given a thousand dollars and left at a shopping mall. Jen had looked at her quizzically, not understanding. "Tell me her story in two thousand words or less." That was two nights ago and Jen had started and restarted the story four times. But she was intrigued by the exercise and Ryan promised to critique it for her. Even though they had satellite, the TV remained off except when Ryan wanted to catch a weather forecast. And even though there was Internet, her own e-mails had been limited. She'd simply sent out a group e-mail, letting everyone know she was okay. She did send a separate one to Brad, telling him she would keep in touch daily but so far, that had not been the case. She realized she had hardly given him a thought the last couple of days. Her time—and thoughts—were occupied elsewhere.

Because their days had taken on a routine as well. She now knew that Ryan was an early riser and normally got up at the ungodly hour of five. By the time Jen crawled out of bed—at a reasonable seven—Ryan had already taken the girls on their first hike of the day. Jen would use that quiet time alone to write in her journal, which had taken on a life of its own. In one of her books, the second one, she'd devoted an entire chapter to the benefits of keeping a journal, of writing down thoughts and dreams. Of course, she'd never done that herself until now, just like she'd never practiced meditation even though she advocated it in each book. She no longer feared getting hacked into tiny pieces by a crazed hermit, but the journal had become therapeutic. This morning she had read back to the first couple of entries and had to laugh. Her trepidation at having to share a bed with someone had been a major concern the first two nights. Now, she no longer hesitated getting into bed. Whether it was because Ryan was a woman or that she simply had no other choice, her phobia of sleeping with someone appeared to have vanished. She did wonder if the same would hold true with Brad. For some reason, she didn't think that would be the case. She folded her arms around herself, glancing at the clock that hung near the kitchen.

She had found that Ryan normally returned by eight so she'd taken on the chore of making breakfast, starting it just a few minutes before Ryan was due back. Breakfast choices were limited as there were no eggs. Ryan had jotted down an easy recipe for biscuits which Jen had made yesterday. She had to admit, they were very good. Ryan's freezer was stocked and today Jen had browned sausage and fried potato slices. If she were in Santa Fe, she'd have fresh, hot tortillas. She had not expected that here, so she was pleasantly surprised to find several packages in the freezer. So, breakfast tacos it was.

As the clock ticked closer to eight thirty, she began to worry. She turned from the window, pacing slowly, her eyes darting between the clock and the door. Should she go out to look for them? *No*. They would be fine. They hiked every morning, regardless of the temperature. Besides, she wouldn't know where to start looking. Ryan had mentioned that they liked to mix up their routes. In the afternoons, Jen had joined them three times so far. Yesterday, it was up the ridge to catch the sunset. It was beautiful, and she wished she'd had her camera. Unfortunately, that too was buried in the avalanche.

She looked again at the clock. Ryan was forty-five minutes late. She felt a touch of panic but pushed it back.

What if something *had* happened to Ryan? What would she do? They had Internet back, but who would she e-mail? And the phone? She assumed Ryan carried her cell with her.

Just as she was about to jump into a full-blown panic attack, the door opened. Her eyes flew to Ryan's, then down her body; she appeared to be unharmed. The dogs ran inside ahead of Ryan, their tongues hanging out as they rushed up to her, nudging her legs. She let out a heavy, relieved breath, smiling at them as they vied for her attention.

"I'm sorry," Ryan said.

Jen raised her eyebrows.

"You looked worried," Ryan explained. "I'm later than normal."

"Oh. Yeah." Jen felt embarrassed now. "I was starting to panic," she admitted.

"We went downhill a little too far. Coming back up took longer than expected," she said as she hung her coat by the door. "Thanks for keeping the stove going."

"I added a log about an hour ago."

Ryan glanced into the kitchen. "Smells good. I hope I haven't ruined it."

"No. I'm sure it's fine. Are you ready to eat?"

Ryan nodded as she held her hands out over the fire. Jen went into the kitchen, surprised by the relief she felt. She hated feeling so dependent on someone, but up here, she was just that. She busied herself with breakfast, feeling Ryan watching her. She finally stopped and looked up, meeting her gaze.

"If there was an emergency, what would you do?" Jen asked her.

"Like what?"

"I mean, what if you got sick or something?"

Ryan shook her head. "I don't get sick. But my first-aid kit is pretty extensive."

"Okay. What if one of the dogs broke her leg?"

"I would set it and she would walk with a limp the rest of her life."

"But what if something major happened? Something life threatening," she said. "What would we do?"

Ryan smiled. "Rule number one—don't panic."

Jen laughed. "If you're the one in danger and you're counting on me to rescue you, you better panic." She placed a plate with a stuffed tortilla on the bar. "Coffee? I made another pot."

"Yes. Please."

Jen filled both of their cups. She knew Ryan liked hers black and she brought it over. To her own, she added a little sugar, then walked around the bar to join her.

"You know, we're not entirely cut off from the world," Ryan reminded her.

"I know. Having e-mail makes me feel a little bit connected, at least."

"Not just that. If there really was a medical emergency, I could call Reese and request a helicopter rescue. There's a search and rescue team in Gunnison," she said. "The bill would be hefty, but in an emergency, we could do it." Ryan took a bite of her taco, and Jen was pleased by the audible moan she heard. "This is great," Ryan said around a mouthful.

"Thanks. It should really have some green chilies, but I made do with some of the red pepper flakes you had." Jen was about to take a bite, then paused. "So if there was no medical emergency but I was willing to pay, they would send a helicopter up to get me?"

Ryan nodded. "Technically, you're a stranded traveler. A consequence of the avalanche."

Jen smiled. "I thought you were going to say, a consequence of me being an idiot."

"I'm sorry I called you an idiot." It was Ryan's turn to pause. "Do you want to get rescued?"

Jen considered the question carefully. If it had been posed to her the first day, the answer would have been a resounding *yes*. She'd have wanted to be rescued and taken back home to Santa Fe, the workshop forgotten. But now, on the sixth day, the answer wasn't quite as conclusive. *Do I want to get rescued?* She supposed, ideally, the answer would be—should be—yes. If for no other reason than that she was infringing on Ryan's space. She decided to flip the question to Ryan.

"Do you want me to get rescued?"

Ryan too seemed to consider the question fully. Jen was pleased by the slight smile that formed. "No. That would mean I'd have to go back to cooking my own breakfast."

"But if I was rescued, you could go back to being a hermit."

"That's true."

"And you wouldn't have to share your bed with someone."

"Well, it's been awhile since a beautiful woman has shared my bed. Certainly never up here. I can't complain about that."

Jen met her eyes briefly, then looked away as a blush threatened. It was an innocent statement meant to tease, yet Jen knew the underlying meaning. Ryan lived alone, in all aspects of her life. She had no...lover. That thought brought the blush wholly to the surface, along with multiple questions.

"Why?"

"Why what?"

"Why are you alone? I mean, I know the hermit thing, but why are you *alone*? You're so...so beautiful." She shook her head, hearing how that sounded. "I mean, attractive." She rolled her eyes. *Is that any better?* "Pretty."

Ryan laughed, seeming to enjoy her discomfort. "Are you asking why don't I have a lover?"

Jen nodded and Ryan's smile left her face.

"I told you, my family is wealthy," Ryan said. "I found that anyone who wanted to get close to me did so because of my family name, nothing more."

"You really believe that?"

"I know that."

"That's sad if you truly believe that, Ryan. I hope that people aren't really that shallow." Jen took a sip of coffee. "Besides, I'm sure you have much more to offer than just your family name, whatever that is. You did, after all, rescue me." Jen rested her elbows on the table, considering Ryan's excuse. "It would be hard to find someone who wanted to live isolated like this, I suppose. But I think you fell in love with someone, and you got hurt. It's easier to lump everyone in the same category then. That way, you won't stand the chance of getting hurt again." Jen met Ryan's eyes, noting the slight flash of anger there, but she didn't pull back.

"You don't know what you're talking about."

"I believe I do."

Ryan pushed her plate away and got up. Jen thought she'd crossed a line and was about to apologize when Ryan held up the coffeepot in a silent offer. Jen nodded. She watched the thoughtful expression on Ryan's face as she poured, wondering if Ryan was about to share some elusive memory with her.

"Her name was Megan. I thought...I thought she was the one, you know." Ryan glanced at her with a smile. "I was young and stupid. Barely twenty. I wanted to offer her the world. Hell, I did. I never quite fit the mold of what my family wanted. What they expected. I hated the dinner parties, the publicity, all of it. Megan, it turned out, loved it all. I wanted to run away. I thought she'd come with me." Ryan met her gaze with a sad smile. "She ran to my brother instead."

"I'm sorry," Jen said quietly.

Ryan shrugged. "She was the first. Not the last."

"Maybe it was the company you kept."

Ryan laughed at that. "Yeah. Maybe I needed to hang with a different crowd, huh?"

"I'm sorry. I don't mean to make light of it," she said, adding sugar to her coffee.

"No, it's okay. I just wanted you to know why I'm alone. Every woman I met, I always wondered if there was an ulterior motive. And there usually was. So, I enjoyed the sex, nothing more." Jen blushed at that and Ryan laughed again. "Sorry. I didn't mean to be so blunt. I forgot about your...upbringing."

Jen nodded, but her curiosity was getting the best of her. "So, are you ever going to tell me your real name?"

"My really, really close friends—of which I have two, Reese and Morgan—call me Ryan. I'd like for you to call me Ryan too."

Jen smiled, pleased by the answer. "Thank you. I feel honored then."

# CHAPTER TEN

"Does it just drop off?"

Ryan leaned on the broom, the fresh, powdery snow all but swept off of the deck. It was warm in the sunshine, and she and Jen had taken off their coats as they shared the task of sweeping snow.

"It's a good drop. But I'd never toss you off here. It's too close to the cabin."

Jen smiled at her but took a step back, away from her. "Your continued mentioning of how to dispose of my body is starting to worry me."

Ryan laughed and walked over to the edge of the deck. She motioned for Jen. "Come here."

Jen hesitated, then moved closer, craning her neck to look over the side. From the cabin windows, it looked like a sheer drop-off into the canyon. It was just an illusion. Ryan leaned casually on the railing, beckoning Jen to join her. This was Jen's first time out on the deck and she wanted her to see the view.

"I have a slight fear of heights," Jen said.

Ryan held her hand out, and Jen took it without question. "It's okay. It doesn't really drop off."

Jen leaned against her as she peered over the side. "Well, now I'm embarrassed."

Below them was another deck, only five feet from the railing. And below that was the slope of the ridge, still another hundred feet or more from the canyon edge.

"I call that the sun deck," Ryan said. She pointed to the side. "Steps are over there."

"It's magnificent. The views are incredible."

Ryan nodded. Besides the guys who built the cabin, only Reese and Morgan had been up there. She was actually thrilled to have someone else appreciate the beauty of it. She felt Jen squeeze her hand before releasing it, and Ryan quickly shoved her own in her pockets. She leaned against the railing with her hip, her gaze sliding back to Jen involuntarily. Jen shielded her eyes from the sun, still perusing the view with a smile on her face. Wisps of blond hair stuck out beneath her wool cap, and her cheeks had a rosy glow to them.

"So beautiful."

Ryan blinked, unaware she'd been staring. She met Jen's eyes briefly. "Yes," she murmured, then shoved off the railing. "Intoxicating, isn't it?"

"Peaceful," Jen countered. "I can't imagine anyone being able to gaze out across the mountains like this and

still harbo
thoughts."

"What?
"Yes. I f
her side. "St
Ryan lau
"Yes. It's
no deadlines,
calls. No nee
No getting lo
"I understa
"Habitually
has something
"Being hom
"Both, I sup

I would pretend to be sick. I woul
headache. When I started my
terrible cramps and couldn'
it on me being a teena
Jen said with a smile
going to turn into
"But that w
Jen lau
no dan
and
h

.... view and
faced Ryan, her ... ...ougurrul. "Each week, Monday
through Saturday, I wouldn't see another soul except my
grandparents. I wasn't allowed to watch TV and the only
radio was controlled by my grandfather. It wasn't until
Sunday at church that I saw—and talked to—other people."

Jen walked slowly along the deck, her hand absently
brushing the snow from the top of the railing. "I told
you I was socially inept. I was also painfully shy. I didn't
know how to talk to people, to other kids. I related
better to adults, I think, because I was always around
adults." She glanced at Ryan briefly. "My clothes were
very, very conservative. Decades old and out of style.
And I had these hideous glasses," she said, pointing at
her face. "The other kids would make fun of me."

Their eyes met, and Ryan saw a host of emotions there.
She didn't know what to say so she kept quiet, waiting on
Jen to continue her story.

"I hated leaving the house. So when Sunday rolled
around, I would delay the inevitable as long as possible. My
grandfather was already at the church, preparing for his
sermon, I guess. That left my grandmother to deal with me.

...d say I had a horrendous
... period, I would say I had
...t get out of bed. They blamed
...er and 'going through a phase,'"
..."I'm certain they were terrified I was
...my mother."

...asn't the case?"

...ghed. "No. I had no friends. They were in
...er of me following in my mother's footsteps
...alling into bad company." She shrugged. "I missed
...ving friends, but I guess I didn't *know* I missed it."

"Hard to miss something you never had?"

"Yes. It wasn't until I was in college and made a few friends that I understood it all. As much as I made fun of the wallflower book I read, it did prompt me to make some changes. In my clothes, mainly." She grinned. "And to tell them my first major lie. I told them I broke my glasses and needed new ones. I conveniently did this on Sunday when I was heading back to Lubbock. I couldn't do without glasses, and even they wouldn't send me out in public with them taped together."

"So they gave you money?" Ryan guessed.

"Yep. And I spent it on contacts instead of glasses. My one and only act of rebellion, for which they were very, very angry with me."

Ryan looked into those blue eyes, wondering if that was the reason for their unique color. Jen must have sensed her question and shook her head.

"No. I had eye surgery," she said. "Lasik. I no longer need contacts or glasses."

"Your eyes are...beautiful," Ryan said quietly. "I'm glad the color is not the result of artificial lenses."

"Thank you. I have my father's eyes. I don't know who he is. My mother claims she doesn't either." Jen turned away. "When I was younger, I always thought that would be how I'd find him. By his eyes."

"I take it he wasn't a member of your church then?"

"No. I asked my mother about him a few years ago. She still claims she has no idea who he is." Jen's gaze traveled back over the snow-covered mountains, and Ryan wondered if her thoughts were as far away as well. "I was apparently conceived at a drug party where she had sex with as many as seven different guys."

Again, Ryan didn't know what to say. For as much as she wanted to run away from her family name, at least she knew who her family was. She had no consoling words to offer Jen, so she said nothing. She heard Jen sigh before she turned back around.

"How in the world did I get off on that subject?"

Ryan gave her what she hoped was a reassuring smile. "You're habitually late."

Jen laughed. "Yes. I'm late and I get lost." She held out both hands and moved them up and down. "It's a right and left thing. I have two lefts, apparently."

"Well, so you don't get lost around here, do you want to go on a hike with us? The wind has died down. This is probably as warm as we can expect it today."

Jen nodded. "Yes. Thank you. I'd like that."

***

Jen struggled to keep up, Ryan and the dogs moving ahead of her on the trail that snaked between the trees. At least, she thought it was a trail. With all the snow, she had no idea how they knew where they were going.

"You okay back there?"

"I'm out of shape."

"It's the altitude."

"Okay," she gasped. "We can use that excuse." Ryan stopped, letting her catch up. Jen grabbed her arm and leaned on her, breathing heavily. "You could at least pretend to be winded," she said.

Ryan laughed, then opened her mouth and gave an exaggerated gasp for air. "How's that?"

"Thank you. I feel so much better now."

"You could come with us every day, you know. By the time you leave here, you could run a marathon."

"Oh yes, that's *always* been a goal of mine," she said with a smirk. "Is this one of your normal routes?"

"Yeah. The snow is not as thick here in the trees. These are mostly ponderosa pines. Up around the cabin, it's mostly spruce and fir," she said. She then pointed to a clearing on their left. "In the summer, that's a beautiful meadow. It's covered in wildflowers. In the evenings, we hike down here and watch the elk grazing."

"They're not scared of the dogs?"

"We don't get that close." She turned, pointing back from where they'd come. "You can't tell it now, but there's a rock outcropping there. We watch from up there."

Jen thought it was amusing that Ryan referred to "we" when talking about herself and the dogs. Of course, when you lived alone and they were your only companions, she supposed their roles in her life were more than that of a pet. She followed Ryan's gaze to Sierra and Kia, seeing the affection in her eyes as she watched them playing like children in the snow. Jen enjoyed their antics too. While her grandparents had had a dog, he wasn't what she would call a pet; he never once set foot inside their house. He wasn't a part of the family, not like Sierra and Kia were.

"Why don't you want to get married?"

Jen looked at Ryan, startled by the question. "Where in the world did that come from?"

Ryan shrugged. "You've been up here nearly two weeks now and you haven't mentioned him since that first time. You know, the guy who wants to marry you?"

Jen laughed. "Brad." Her smile faded. "We've e-mailed twice. Shouldn't that tell us something?" She didn't really want to talk about Brad. If they did, she would start dissecting their relationship—again—trying to put her finger on what was troubling her. Truth was, the month-long workshop, being sequestered, so to speak, was not only to hone her skills at writing. It was also going to afford her some alone time to examine and truly assess her feelings for Brad.

"So what's the deal?"

Jen pulled her cap off and tousled her hair. Standing in the sun like they were, it was almost balmy. She turned her gaze to Ryan, putting voice to her thoughts. "I'm afraid."

Ryan nodded. "You want to talk about it?"

Jen gave her a quick smile as she twisted her cap between her fingers. "I don't know if it's...real," she said. "I don't know...I mean, how do you know if you're truly in love with someone? Shouldn't there be more than this?"

"More than what?"

She shrugged. "I don't know. I just feel like—and this is so adolescent—but there are no fireworks," she said, embarrassed by the direction of their conversation.

"No Fourth of July when he kisses you?"

Jen smiled and turned away from her. "No. But I don't know if that's what I mean. It's just, it seems like there should be *more*. So I don't know if it's me, or if this is all there is." She shrugged again. "Maybe there isn't more. But if there is, then this isn't what I want." She laughed. "I know I'm not making any sense," she said. She turned, meeting Ryan's eyes expectantly. "I want more."

"Well, I'm certainly no expert on relationships," Ryan said. "My experience is with Megan, remember. But if you're questioning it, then I'd guess that you're not in love with him."

"In love. That's so ambiguous, isn't it?" She pulled her gaze from Ryan, scanning the white terrain around them instead. "Brad and I were friends," she said. "There was never any hint of...of sexual feelings between us. At least, not for me. We were just friends. I don't even remember when or how we started dating. In fact, I think we had two or three or even four dates before he kissed me." She looked back at Ryan, wondering why she was acknowledging the failings of her relationship to her. "It wasn't...it wasn't spectacular. But there was nothing else for me. Certainly nothing for me to compare it to. He was it. I think I was afraid of other guys. I was afraid of the uncertainty of it. Brad was safe. I knew Brad, I knew what to expect. Back then, that was important to me." Sierra leaned against her leg and she reached down, ruffling her dark fur. "I had been so sheltered, I needed that safety net," she said. "But I've changed so much since then. I've grown. I'm not the same person. And I don't think he's who I want to spend the rest of my life with." As soon as she said the words out loud, she knew they were true. She smiled sadly. "I guess I just answered my own question. I love him. I care about him." She took a deep breath, letting it out slowly. "I'm just not *in* love with him. I can't marry him."

"Have you told him any of this?"

"No. Not quite so bluntly. I have questioned him as to whether he's sure he's happy with me. He says he is."

"Has he asked if you're happy with him?"

Jen shook her head. "I guess he just assumes that I am. I wouldn't say that I'm terribly unhappy," she said. "I think I've just been content with it all." She met Ryan's steady gaze, holding it. "I don't miss him. I don't miss that familiarity of having him in my life. I don't miss our phone calls. I don't miss our dinner dates. What I do miss is the friendship we had way back when."

"If you're not happy, you should tell him before he pops the question. Then it's just going to get awkward."

"I know. I haven't known what to tell him until now," she admitted. "I think, being out here, away from everything, away from our friends, put it in perspective. All of our friends are mutual. All of them. I couldn't talk to any of them. Well, except Cheryl. She's my closest friend. She works at Anasazi Press. That's where I met her." Jen smiled.

"Back then, when I first started there, I was terribly shy. It's a miracle I made it through the interview," she said with a quick laugh. "I had a really hard time talking to people. But anyway, I think she suspects that I'm not happy. She knows I don't want to get married." She pictured Cheryl's easy smile; she was one of the few people she actually did miss.

"So I guess getting stuck by an avalanche has had some benefit then," Ryan said with a smile.

"For me, yes. I don't know what you're getting out of it though."

"Besides breakfast, you mean?"

"Well, there's that," she said.

"Oh, it hasn't been bad," Ryan said. "I have actually enjoyed your company."

Jen was surprised by that statement. Pleasantly surprised. During the first few days, she was certain Ryan was cursing herself for rescuing her. But now, two weeks later, they'd settled into an easy friendship. At least, for her it was easy.

"Thank you. And for being a hermit and someone who doesn't like people, you've been a most excellent host."

Their conversation was interrupted by a chattering squirrel perched on a pine limb. Jen couldn't tell if it was fussing at them or the dogs. "It's beautiful. What kind is it?"

"Abert's squirrel," Ryan said. "Or tassel-eared, as it's most commonly called. We've apparently interrupted lunch." Ryan started walking again, and the dogs immediately ran ahead of her. Jen followed, glancing back once to look at the squirrel, which continued its tirade.

# CHAPTER ELEVEN

Jen was tapping away on her laptop. Ryan watched, staring as Jen's lips lifted in a smile. Her curiosity got the best of her.

"Are you still working on the exercise I gave you?"

Jen shook her head. "Oh, I finished that. I'm just writing in my journal."

"A journal, huh?"

"Yes." Jen glanced at her and shook her head again. "And, no, you may not read it."

"Wouldn't dream of asking," she said. "How about your story?"

Jen's fingers stilled, and she was quiet for a long moment. "It's not very good," she finally said. "That's why I never told you I finished it. I must have started over five times."

Ryan nodded. "I want to read it later, but first I want you to tell me about it."

"What do you mean? I thought you were going to critique it. You know, my first writing exercise," Jen reminded her.

"I will. But I want to get your verbal take on it."

Jen closed her laptop and tucked her feet under her. Ryan closed hers as well, giving Jen her full attention.

"Okay. I admit it, I had a really hard time with it," Jen said. "It sounded simple enough when you gave it to me. I mean, shopping spree, how hard can that be?"

"But?"

"But I did like you said. I made her a real person, with a real family. And I told her story."

"So tell me."

"Well, first thing she did was...oh, and I named her Carla," Jen said. "First thing Carla wanted to buy were clothes. New clothes. She'd always had hand-me-downs. She was the youngest of four sisters. So she goes into this expensive shop and is shocked by the prices. She is almost afraid to touch anything. She knows that the thousand dollars won't go far in there, so she leaves and ends up at a department store. The prices are better, and she finds several things she wants. But each time she picks something up, she thinks that her sisters would like it too and it would be unfair for her to go home with new clothes. So she doesn't buy any clothes. Then she thinks...jewelry. She's wearing cheap, over-the-counter earrings, and she sees some pretty gold ones, even some with diamonds. She still can't justify buying them. She goes to all these different stores, looks at all the things she doesn't have and wishes she did. But she doesn't buy a thing. She finally leaves the mall with nothing. Except the thousand dollars." Jen looked at her expectantly. "Silly, right? I mean, that I couldn't decide what to buy."

"Not silly at all. The point of that exercise is to tell you something about yourself. You'd be surprised at how often the story reflects the personality of the writer, despite it being fiction. So what did Carla do with the money?"

"I don't know. Maybe she gave it to her parents to help with bills. Maybe she split it up between her sisters. Or maybe she put it in a savings account for college," Jen said with smile. "That would be the sensible thing to do."

"And the least fun."

"So where did you come up with that exercise?"

"It was something a professor did when I was in college." As soon as she said that, she saw questions forming in Jen's eyes.

"What—" But Jen shook her head. "No. Never mind."

Ryan laughed. "Was that hard to do? To not ask your question?"

"Yeah. But I've decided that you have a right to your privacy and if you don't want to talk to me about anything personal, then that's your business. I'm not going to bombard you with questions anytime you do let something slip. Like college," she added with a smile.

"I'm just not used to talking about myself," she said. "Talking period."

"That's fine," Jen said, feigning disinterest.

Ryan watched her as she appeared absorbed in reading. She was surprised by the words that spilled out from her. "I've been here two years. Before that, I bought an old mining shack at the edge of Aspen. Spent a couple of years fixing it up. But it wasn't really isolated. Not like here."

Jen didn't move or lift her eyes, almost as if she was afraid to move, lest Ryan stop talking.

"I ran into my brother and his entourage on a ski slope one year and decided it was time to move on."

At this, Jen did lift her head. "Are you estranged from your family?"

"I don't know if I would call it that," she said. "We had a bit of a falling out about ten years ago."

"But you still talk to them? See them?"

"Talk to them? No, not really," she said with a shake of her head. "I see them. Occasionally." Because she had obligations, she reminded herself.

"But you're not estranged?"

Ryan grinned. "That word just seems so melodramatic."

Jen nodded but didn't ask anything else about her family. "Why here? Why Lake City?" she asked instead.

"Aspen was...busy. But I wasn't—" *Wasn't writing.* "I wasn't working," she said.

"No editing gig there?"

Ryan shook her head. "I wanted someplace where I didn't have to worry about tourists everywhere but also someplace where I could venture into civilization if I wanted."

"Again, some hermit you are."

Ryan was tempted to tell her the whole sordid tale but knew, after this much time, that Jen would probably be pissed to learn she was a writer. Not just a writer, but a Pulitzer Prize winner. Of course, Jen might remember the tabloid stories or have heard them, since she was in the business. She might even be one of those who believed a ghostwriter had actually penned the book. After all, her own family did. *Does.* Thank goodness, the Pulitzer committee didn't. They had accepted the proofs she'd presented of her authorship, which had averted the disgrace of having them rescind the award. So no, she certainly did not want to hash all that over again. She stood, taking her laptop to her desk, ending the conversation.

"I'm going to take the dogs out."

\*\*\*

Ryan pulled the covers back on the bed, debating whether to turn the lamp off or not. Jen was in the bathroom and had been for an unusually long time. Of course, maybe she was simply avoiding her. Her mood had turned sour, she knew, and she'd stay out with the dogs longer than normal. When she returned, Jen had looked at her warily and Ryan hadn't explained—or commented on—her abruptness. Thinking about that time in her life always put her in a funk. The betrayal of her family and their total lack of interest in the truth still smarted. She could still hear her mother's laugh when one of countless reporters had questioned her. "A writer? Catherine? Don't be ridiculous." *Right*, she thought. Catherine Ryan-Barrett couldn't possibly be talented enough to write a novel. She was an heiress with literary pretensions, nothing more. The tabloids ate it up, and her own mother kept stoking the fire. Any publicity was good publicity, as far as her mother was concerned.

She shook those thoughts away, knowing she had to quit dwelling on them. That had happened a lifetime ago. She needed to live in the present. And right now, that meant checking on her guest.

She paused at the bathroom door, listening. She heard nothing and knocked twice, softly.

"Jen? You okay?"

The door opened slowly, and Jen stood there, tears in her eyes. Ryan frowned, startled by the tears.

"What's wrong?"

Jen looked down at the floor. "I started my period."

Ryan hid her smile, not understanding. "I am a woman, you know. I'm familiar with it."

Jen's chest heaved with a sob. "I only have one tampon."

Without thinking, Ryan pulled her into a hug, which only caused more tears. Jen buried her face against Ryan's chest as she clung to her. It struck her that this was the first physical contact she'd had with anyone in more months than she could remember. It felt good to hold another woman again. Of course, she realized how terribly inappropriate that thought was.

"I have plenty," Ryan said. "It's no problem."

"Yes it is. I'm eating your food. I'm taking up your space. And now I have to bum tampons from you."

"And all of that is okay."

"I'm sorry," Jen murmured. "It just all hit me, I guess."

Ryan squeezed her tightly, then pulled away. She tipped Jen's head up with a finger under her chin, those beautiful blue eyes still swimming in tears. Involuntarily, her gaze drifted to Jen's mouth, and she felt a jolt of arousal. She dropped her hand and stepped away, embarrassed.

Without another word, she went back to the bedroom and clicked off the lamp. Just a few minutes later, Jen came in, pausing at the edge of the bed. *Great. Now she's scared of me again.* There was enough moonlight shining in that Ryan could make out her features. She looked like a goddess. After what seemed an eternally long time, Jen moved to her side of the bed. She quietly lifted up the covers, took off her sweatpants, then got in.

Ryan felt like a heel; she didn't know what to say. "I'm sorry."

"You don't have to apologize," Jen said, her voice quiet in the dark room. "Your past is your past and it's of no concern to me. It's shaped who you are, but it's still the past. If that's what you're running from, it's not any of my business."

Ryan smiled into the darkness. Innocent Jen had no idea how that hug had affected her. It was just as well. Jen turned her head, looking at her, but there wasn't enough light for Ryan to read her features.

"The only thing that's important is right now," Jen continued. "And the future. So if you don't ever want to mention anything about your past again, that's fine with me."

"I appreciate that. Although I wasn't really apologizing for my abruptness this afternoon. I was apologizing for... well, for hugging you."

"Why would you need to apologize for that? I was having a...a moment," Jen said with a slight laugh. "I needed a hug."

"A moment, huh? Should I be worried?"

Jen rolled to her side and faced her. "Can I tell you something?"

"Of course."

"I've never slept with anyone before. I mean, I haven't been *able* to sleep with anyone, share a bed." She paused for a moment, then continued, her voice quiet. "When I was a kid, at my grandparents' house, I was the only one. I was homeschooled, I didn't have friends. There were no sleepovers, slumber parties. And in college, I lived with Miss Ruby. She—"

"The bitter old woman who never smiled?"

"Yes, that one. I certainly never had anyone over there. I lived with her for four years. From there, I moved to Santa Fe. Got my own place."

"So...Brad?"

"No. I mean, we tried, but—"

"Never?"

"I can't sleep. I don't want to call it an anxiety attack, but maybe that's what it is. I can't sleep. I can't even close my eyes. It's just strange having him in bed, having *anyone* in bed with me."

"That must put a damper on your sex life," she said, although she didn't really want to talk about Jen's sex life.

Jen sighed. "We don't have much of a sex life as it is, so yes, that does have an effect on it. But I just find it odd that I don't have that same anxiety with you."

"The first couple of nights, you weren't exactly bounding into bed," she reminded her.

Jen laughed. "The first night I think I was more worried about you hacking me into little pieces than I was sleeping with you."

"And you're over that now, I hope."

"Yes. It's actually kinda nice sleeping with someone."

"We'll see there. When you get back home, maybe you can give Brad another try."

Jen only sighed and rolled again to her back. "Maybe."

# CHAPTER TWELVE

"I can't believe how warm it is," Jen said. She turned in a circle, arms held out from her sides. "I mean, clear skies, nothing but sunshine." She smiled and tilted her head. "Listen. You can actually hear the snow melting."

"Yes. The wonderful signs of spring," she said. They'd left their coats at the cabin. She had a sweatshirt on over her shirt. Jen wore one of the two sweaters she had.

"Are you *sure* a storm is coming?"

"Spring blizzards aren't uncommon," she said. "Twenty-four hours or so of a winter blast, then this again. The sounds of it all melting." She eyed Jen who had a wistful look on her face. "It shouldn't delay you getting out of here," she said.

Jen turned to her. "Oh, I wasn't worried about that. I was thinking about sledding."

"Sledding?"

"All this snow. It's like a giant playground." Jen reached down to pet Sierra, who was leaning against her leg. Kia was normally the more affectionate dog, but Ryan had noticed that Sierra had taken a liking to Jen. "I've never played in the snow before," Jen said.

Their daily hikes had taken them all over the mountain and never once had it occurred to her to play. Jen had been here four weeks now, going on five, and while she never mentioned leaving, Ryan assumed she still counted down the days. She still wrote in her journal, in great detail of their daily activities, Jen said. She wondered how long she had been harboring the desire to play in the snow.

"I don't have a sled," she said. "But I think we can find something to use."

Jen's eyes lit up. "Really?"

"Yeah, sure. Let's bring enough firewood inside to last through the storm. Then we'll go out to the shed and see what we can find."

Jen smiled brightly. "Thank you. That'd be fun."

A little over an hour later, with the sun still shining brightly, Ryan looked skeptically at the piece of plywood she'd commandeered for their sled. She'd drilled two holes in the front and slipped a rope through, but still, it was rudimentary at best.

"Maybe I should take it on a test spin and make sure I don't kill us," she suggested.

"Oh, it looks fine," Jen said, grinning like a child. "Besides, this is a little hill. If it works, I want to go on a really big hill."

Ryan laughed. "Don't forget, you still have to climb back up that really big hill."

She sat down on the plywood and spread her legs, digging the heels of her boots into the snow. Kia licked her face and tried to lay down in front of her. "No, no, no. You don't get to go," she said, nudging her out of the way. She held her hand out to Jen.

"I've never done this before," Jen warned.

"I know. You'll do fine."

Jen settled down between her legs, scooting back tight against her. Ryan put her arms around Jen's waist, feeling Jen grab them to pull them even tighter together. *God.* She took a deep breath, then took the rope, hoping to use it to help them stop.

"Ready?"

Jen nodded vigorously, and Ryan noted the anticipation on her face.

"Okay. Hang on."

She wrapped her legs around Jen and shoved off. They were soon racing down the hill. Jen screamed with pleasure as she held tight to Ryan's arms. The dogs, she was certain, had no clue as to their antics, but they ran behind them, barking joyfully as they tried to catch them. Even she had to admit that it was thrilling racing down the hill as they were. Whether it was from the ride or the woman nestled between her legs, she wasn't sure. But all too soon, it leveled out, and she pulled up on the rope, slowing their speed. Jen leaned back against her, laughing delightfully.

"Oh, *man*, that was fun," Jen said. She looked back at her, her eyes bright. "Can we go again?"

Yeah, it was great fun, Ryan admitted. She laughed too, feeling a bit like a child herself. "Sure, we can go again. As much as you like."

"You shouldn't have said that," Jen said as she got off the sled. She held a hand out to Ryan to help her up, then took the rope, pulling the sled behind her.

The hill was steeper going back up than it appeared, and even she was a bit out of breath by the time they got back to the top. Jen leaned over to catch her breath, still smiling.

"You were right. Going down is great, but you still have to climb back up."

"That's why after two or three, you'll be done."

Jen stood back up and took another couple deep breaths. "I feel great. Can I be in the back this time?"

"You sure?"

"Yeah. Are you afraid I'll spill us?"

Ryan shrugged. "A little tumble in the snow never hurt anyone," she said. Although she wasn't sure if that was her reason for hesitating or not. She glanced at Jen, who was already seated, her legs spread invitingly. Ryan looked away with a slight roll of her eyes. *You're a pig.* She got down, feeling Jen pull her closer as she wrapped her hands around Ryan's waist.

"I'll take care of the rope," she said.

"Good. Because I can barely reach around you," Jen said, scooting up closer to her.

Ryan bit down on her lip, loving—and hating—the feeling of Jen nestled up behind her. If she let her imagination run just a little, she could swear she felt Jen's nipples against her back. "Try not to lean to either side," Ryan cautioned.

"Okay. You ready?"

"Let's go."

They both leaned forward as Jen used her feet to push them off, then she wrapped her legs around Ryan's as they sped down the hill for the second time. Ryan barely had time to register Jen's arms and legs around her before she felt them tipping. She tried to right the makeshift sled but to no avail. They were thrown off, both crashing into the snow as the sled continued down the hill without them.

She spit snow out of her mouth and wiped her face, looking around for Jen. Jen was sitting up, a mixture of panic and joy on her face.

"I'm so sorry," she said. "I leaned." Then she burst into laughter. "That was fun."

Ryan sat back, the dogs dancing around them, licking at their faces. "We're okay," she murmured, petting them both. "Well, like I said, a tumble in the snow never hurt anyone."

"Can we go again?"

"Sure. Just as soon as you go down and fetch the sled."

Jen stuck her tongue out at her playfully, then grinned mischievously as she tossed a snowball at her. Ryan laughed as Jen sprinted away from her. She ruffled the dogs' fur, then stood, watching Jen's progress as she went after their sled. She realized she was still smiling and looked away. Yes, she admitted, she was attracted to Jen. A lot. Sure, Jen was cute and had those killer blue eyes, but she would attribute it more to them being stuck together than anything else. Straight women with fiancés in the picture never had done much to her libido before. As for Jen, their close contact on the sled didn't seem to have affected her in the least. Which she supposed was a good thing. At least Jen wasn't shying away from her.

Jen's breathing was labored as she approached, dragging the sled behind her. The snow was crunchy under her boots and was starting to cake on them.

"Okay. I'm good for one more," Jen said between breaths. "But you're in the back."

"You got it."

Once back at the top of the hill, Ryan steadied the sled. She opened her legs and patted the spot between them. Jen sat down, reaching for Ryan's hands. She pulled them tight around her, holding them in place. Ryan scooted down, pressing Jen snugly between her thighs. *God, that feels good.* She hesitated just a second, relishing it for a moment longer. Jen turned and their eyes met. Ryan was shocked by what she saw there. Her gaze dropped to Jen's lips, then back up.

"Hang on," she said quietly.

Jen nodded, finally ending their intense stare. It was almost in slow motion—their trip down the hill. Ryan could hear each heartbeat, could feel her skin burning where Jen touched it. And with each bump, Jen was slammed back against her, causing her arousal to grow even more. Who would have thought sledding could be an erotic sport? She forced herself to concentrate on keeping them upright, all the while holding Jen tightly in her arms. As they neared the bottom, she loosened her grip, reaching for the rope. She pulled up sharply and dropped her feet, easing them to a clean stop.

She felt Jen quietly laughing against her chest, and she joined in. Jen turned, smiling into her eyes.

"Thank you."

"Oh, it was my pleasure," Ryan said. She wiggled her eyebrows teasingly. "Believe me."

Jen laughed outright. "You're terrible," she said, pushing against her playfully. She got up, holding a hand out for Ryan. As Ryan stood, their eyes held again. "I have never had so much fun," Jen said.

"Yeah?"

"I'm not talking about just today, although this was super. I know me being stuck here wasn't in your plans," Jen said, "and I'm really sorry for that. But I've just had so much *fun* with you. I feel...I don't know, I can't even explain it."

She surprised Ryan by pulling her into a hug. Ryan sunk into the embrace, holding her tightly for a few seconds, again relishing the feeling of having another woman in her arms. When they pulled apart, she was surprised by the subtle blush on Jen's face. She was even more surprised by the look that still lingered in her eyes.

They were both quiet as they trudged back to the cabin. The dogs ran ahead of them, as usual, although their steps were a bit slower too. Apparently their racing up and down the hill had tuckered them as well. To the west, dark clouds were building. Ryan pointed to them.

"Storm's on the horizon," she said.

"How long before it gets here?"

"We should see snow by dusk," she said. "Although the news said the brunt of it wouldn't hit until around midnight."

"So in the morning, this will all be covered again," Jen said as she stopped, her gaze fixed on the dark clouds.

"Blizzard, so yeah. We could get five feet or so. But this time of year, it won't last long. A couple of days and we'll hear it melting again." She paused. "I suppose you're anxious to get out of here, huh?"

Jen had a thoughtful expression on her face as she turned to look at her. "I imagine *you* are more anxious than I." She turned her gaze back to the storm clouds. "This has been...therapeutic for me, I think." Jen smiled then. "Of course, it's been at your expense. I do know my time is dwindling down and I'll be leaving soon. But it hasn't been a hardship for me." She turned to look at her again. "You've been wonderful. I can't thank you enough."

"No need. While the prospect of spending six to eight weeks together was a bit daunting in the beginning, the time has flown by."

"Yes, but I've gotten in your way."

"You haven't been in the way," Ryan insisted.

"No? I doubt you've been working as much as you should. You must have a deadline," Jen said. "Instead, you've been keeping me entertained."

Ryan looked away. No, she hadn't been writing as much but not because Jen was in the way. It was just conversation got in the way, which wasn't a bad thing. But she probably did owe her some kind of explanation about her supposed editing gig.

"I have another few weeks before my deadline," she said. "I'm all but done anyway," she lied.

Jen tilted her head as if studying her—scrutinizing her—and Ryan wondered if Jen knew she was lying. She shifted uncomfortably under her gaze, finally pulling her eyes away as she reached a hand out for Kia.

"My turn to cook dinner," Jen said. "How about stew? We still have potatoes."

"Sounds great," she said, smiling at Jen's casual use of "we." "I'll let you have the shower first. I need to go close up the shed and cover the firewood pile and tend to a few other things before the snow falls."

Jen nodded and headed to the cabin. Ryan watched her for a moment, then turned, whistling for the dogs as she made her way around the side and to the shed.

# CHAPTER THIRTEEN

Jen stood at the window, watching the first snowflakes fall lazily to the deck. The storm had rolled in quickly, the dark clouds hiding the sun, bringing an abrupt end to the day. The stew was simmering and the aroma was filling up the cabin, making for a cozy evening. Ryan had taken the dogs out on a short hike before dark, leaving Jen alone with her increasingly unsettled thoughts.

She didn't quite know what to make of it all. Her growing attachment to Ryan was one thing, but something else, just under the surface, was clamoring to be heard. She'd felt it for days, if not weeks, yet it wasn't until the sled ride that she truly understood it. And if she'd had the energy to hike up the hill again, she'd have requested just one more ride, just to feel that thrill. Not the excitement of speeding on the snow, but the thrill of being cushioned in Ryan's arms, held tight against her body.

She turned away from the window, her face flushed, embarrassed by her thoughts. She wasn't comfortable around most people, and she wasn't one for touching or being touched. She wasn't a hugger. At first, she hadn't grasped the concept of sledding. When Ryan had beckoned her to sit between her legs, she should have objected. Their personal space would be blurred. Turns out, not only was it blurred, it was totally erased. The pleasure she felt as those arms snaked around her waist was immense. And she wanted to try it, she wanted to be the one in the back, she wanted to know what it felt like to touch someone that way.

She smiled shyly. She had been so distracted by holding Ryan against her the way she had, she had completely forgotten about sledding and ended up toppling them over. Which was fun in itself.

Fun. Yes, the day had been fun. And full of surprises. And now a blizzard was approaching and they were safe and warm inside. Ryan had said they needed to conserve their power usage so they didn't drain the batteries, but she did turn the TV on long enough to catch a weather forecast. The high mountains could get five feet or more of snow, certainly enough to cover their solar panels and bury the satellite dish.

She glanced at her laptop, fully charged. They still had Internet. She supposed she should catch up on her e-mail, but she ignored that task, as she had been doing lately. She e-mailed Cheryl at least once a week, just to let her know she was okay. She and Brad had exchanged only a few short notes. And Susan, her agent, she'd e-mailed twice. But yesterday when she'd checked her mail, she had ten or twelve that needed her attention and it was just too overwhelming. She'd closed her laptop and ignored them, including one from Brad she had yet to even read.

She heard a bark outside and knew they were back. She went into the kitchen to stir the stew, stirring her own thoughts as well.

"It's started," Ryan said unnecessarily, as the evidence littered her dark hair. "The wind's picking up too."

Jen's gaze followed her to the stove where she held her hands out to warm them. There was only one small lamp on, making it appear even later than it was.

"Has the temperature dropped?" she asked. It had been almost spring-like during their sledding.

Ryan nodded. "Yeah, the front is definitely here." She made a show of sniffing the air. "Smells great. I'm starving."

"Must have been all that sledding you did," she teased.

"Must have been." Ryan joined her in the kitchen, lifting the lid and sniffing again. "Mmm. Can I help with something?" Ryan offered.

"No. It just needs to simmer another half hour or so."

"Was that the last of the potatoes?"

"Afraid so."

"So it's on to rice then, I guess. When Reese comes to get you, I need to request a care package."

Their eyes met briefly, then they both pulled away. Yes, she knew their time together was coming to an end. She'd known it when they'd been out playing. The snow was melting so fast. Yet there would be a reprieve, thanks to the blizzard. Jen turned away, shocked that she was actually thankful for the storm. No doubt Ryan was more than ready for the spring thaw.

"What do you think? Another couple of weeks?"

Ryan nodded. "If the temperature pops back up, I'd guess another week to ten days."

Jen forced a smile to her face. "See? I'll be out of your hair in no time."

"Yes, but I'm getting spoiled by your cooking. I'll have to fend for myself again."

Jen followed her movement as Ryan walked to the windows, looking out into the darkness. Jen wondered what she was thinking about. She saw her take a deep breath, then let it out heavily. As Ryan moved, Jen looked away, making a show of stirring the stew.

Conversation lagged as Ryan settled in her recliner with her laptop. The dogs were sprawled out on the floor beside her, creating a scene Jen would remember fondly, she was sure. She let her eyes travel over them, landing on Ryan, noting her disheveled hair, her nearly flawless skin, hands that were both soft and strong, fingers long and limber, the nails neatly trimmed. Jen's gaze drifted back to her face, Ryan's brows were drawn, her lips somewhat parted, moving ever so slightly as she read. She was disarmingly attractive, and Jen wondered again why she was alone. She wished Ryan trusted her enough to divulge more about her past. Jen had talked freely about her life, yet Ryan had revealed so little.

"What thoughts are running through that pretty head of yours?"

Jen blinked, realizing that she had been staring. She shook her head and smiled. "Private thoughts." She took two bowls out, pausing to stir the stew one more time. "Ready to eat?"

"Yes. Let me help," Ryan said, getting up from her recliner.

"I've got it. What would you like to drink?"

"I've got a few bottles of wine saved back," Ryan said. "Not sure how well they will go with stew, though."

"I wouldn't know the difference," she said. "I don't know the first thing about wine."

And she didn't, she thought, as she took a sip. The red wine was a bit dry for her, but Ryan seemed pleased with it. Ryan also dug into the stew, which in turn, pleased her.

"Very good," Ryan said after another bite. "I've never really tried to cook a stew before. When I want soup or something, I usually just open a can."

"Thanks. My grandmother was big on soup and stew. We had one or the other at least once a week."

"You'll have to give me pointers before you leave then," Ryan said. "My cooking experience has been trial and error. It's not something I learned to do growing up."

Jen ignored the reference to her leaving and instead used Ryan's brief statement to ask a question she'd been curious about. "Where did you grow up?"

Ryan was quiet for the longest time, and Jen thought she wasn't going to answer. But finally, with an almost apologetic smile, she said, "The Hamptons."

Jen's eyebrows shot up. "Really?"

Ryan shrugged. "Mostly."

Which, of course, brought more questions to mind, but the look on Ryan's face told her to keep them to herself. Which she did. The rest of the meal was eaten in near silence with only an occasional comment about the weather each time a gust of wind rattled the windows. It was a bit exciting to know that a major blizzard was happening outside yet they were comfy and warm inside, with no worries of being stranded. Well, no more than they already were.

Ryan helped her clean up the kitchen after dinner, but again, it was a mostly silent affair. She wondered at Ryan's mood. Even for her, she was being extremely quiet this evening.

However, their routine didn't waiver as they both took their respective seats with laptops in hand. Ryan immediately began tapping away, and Jen opened up her journal. Feeling a bit shy as she wrote down her thoughts from earlier, recounting their adventure on the sled, she nonetheless went into great detail. Knowing she would be leaving soon, she figured she would delve into it all again once she was back home...and alone.

At nine, Ryan closed up her laptop and stood, stretching her arms over her head with a satisfied sigh. Jen found her gaze traveling up Ryan's body. She turned away quickly when she found her eyes glued to Ryan's breasts. She felt the temperature in the room rise twenty degrees, and she reached for her glass of water, downing it in one gulp.

"Gonna take the girls out one more time before bed," Ryan said.

Jen nodded. Ryan was already putting on her coat and gloves, both dogs dancing around her excitedly. She left without another word, and Jen finally released her breath. She leaned back, wondering what was happening to her.

She stared out through the dark window for several minutes, her thoughts still a jumbled mess. With a sigh, she stood, placing her laptop next to Ryan's on the small desk. She went through her nighttime routine by rote, pausing to meet her reflection in the mirror a time or two but refusing to dwell on her thoughts, refusing to explore why her gaze had been fixed on Ryan's breasts.

A strong gust of wind shook the cabin, and she involuntarily wrapped her arms around herself. She glanced at the clock, noting that Ryan had been gone nearly thirty minutes. While that wouldn't cause a concern on most nights, it seemed an abnormally long time for them to be out during a blizzard.

Another ten minutes had her pacing with worry, her glance shifting between the clock and the back door. Her fear and apprehension increased with each tick of the clock. She tried to quell the uneasiness that settled over her, but she was barely able to keep panic at bay.

What if something had happened to them? What if Ryan was hurt?

Her fear overrode her good sense as she hurried to the door, pulling her coat on quickly. As soon as she opened the door, swirling snow enveloped her, the wind taking her breath away as she walked into the cold, dark night.

"Ryan!" she yelled, but the roar of the storm carried the sound away immediately. "Ryan!"

She turned in a circle, getting her bearings. The hulk of the cabin was barely visible in the blowing snow. She looked on the ground, trying to find footprints, but the drifting snow made that impossible.

"Sierra! Kia!" Her panic now had a firm grip on her, and she nearly choked on her own voice. "Ryan!"

A fierce gust of wind made her stumble, and she caught herself before she fell. She squinted through the snow, looking in all directions, but she could no longer make out the cabin. Now alarmed, she took deep breaths, trying to calm herself. She couldn't be more than twenty or thirty feet from the cabin. Logically, she should be able to find it.

"Logically," she muttered. "One, two, three, four, five," she counted as she walked, stopping at fifteen. Still no view of the cabin. She turned, retracing her steps, then started all over again, going in a different direction. Still nothing.

She glanced up, hoping for a break in the storm, hoping for a little light from the moon. All she saw was swirling, blinding snow. She finally gave in to her fear, the weight of it settling on her chest and nearly choking her. She walked blindly into the night, hands held out as she waded into the white abyss.

# CHAPTER FOURTEEN

"I hope you know where you're going," Ryan said, following the dogs. At least she'd had the foresight to take their leashes. She knew enough about the dangers of a blizzard to know she shouldn't have been out in it, but cabin fever had a grip on both her and the dogs.

That and the need she felt to put some space between herself and Jen. So okay, sure, she was attracted to her. She'd already admitted that. But it was something she'd managed to keep at bay, hidden below the surface. It was something she could ignore.

*Until that damn sled ride.*

It reared its ugly head then, screaming to be heard. And she heard it loud and clear. Unfortunately, so did Jen. Ryan could see the bewilderment in Jen's eyes when she looked at her. She could see the confusion Jen apparently felt. Hell, it was inevitable, she supposed. They were stuck here together, alone. It stood to reason that they would grow close. And they had. They had grown *too* close. They were too comfortable with each other. So much so that Ryan fought with herself daily to keep her past bottled up, fighting not to blurt out all the sordid details to Jen. She no longer feared Jen would judge her. What she now feared was that too much time had passed. Jen had talked freely about writing and about her desire to produce a novel. If Jen knew who she was, she would be angry and hurt that she hadn't told her...and then she would be embarrassed. And Ryan didn't want her to feel embarrassed about her enthusiasm for writing.

She stopped up short when she realized the dogs had led her safely back to the cabin. She unhooked their leashes, then opened the door, letting them run inside ahead of her as she stomped her boots on the mat.

"Hey, sorry we were so long," she said, looking around for Jen and not seeing her. "Jen?" she called as she slipped her coat off. She didn't think Jen would have gone to bed without waiting for them to return, but maybe she was tired. She held her hands out to the stove, her glance going to the closed bathroom door. The dogs looked at her expectantly, neither quieting down for the night, and she felt an uneasiness settle over her.

"Jen?"

She opened the bathroom door, finding it empty. A glance into the bedroom confirmed her fear. "Jen?" She hurried to the back door, groaning at what she didn't see— Jen's coat. She hadn't even noticed it was missing when she'd hung her own on the rack.

She grabbed the leashes off of the peg, not needing to call the girls as they both seemed to know what was going on. She fumbled with the hooks, her nervousness wreaking havoc with her senses. She slipped her coat on, then back out into the storm they went. Ryan trusted the dogs' instincts as they headed off in the opposite direction of their earlier hike.

"Jen!" she yelled, only to have her words carried away by the wind.

The dogs tugged at her arms, and she nearly had to run to keep up with them. She could see nothing in the blowing snow and hoped the dogs had a sense of what they were looking for. They moved with a purpose, so different than their normal hikes. Amazingly, they seemed to know what this trek out into the blizzard was for.

Sharp warning barks sounded, and Ryan stopped short, her heart catching in her throat at what she saw. Jen lay face down, her coat almost buried by the blowing snow. Ryan fell to her knees, her heart pounding so loudly she could barely breathe.

"Jen? Oh God, please," she murmured as she turned her over. "Jen," she said, taking off a glove and patting her face. It was cold. So cold. She pulled her head up, her mouth directly on Jen's ear. "Jen, wake up. Please. Wake up." She patted her face, relieved to see Jen's eyelids open, but her gaze was unfocused. She patted her face again. "Stay with me."

"Tired," Jen mumbled.

"No, no. Please, Jen. Stay with me," she said as she struggled to stand. "I'm taking you home." She put her glove back on, then, as if Jen weighed little more than a sack of dog food, she tossed her over her shoulder. She wrapped the leashes around her hand, then followed the dogs again. "Home."

The dogs fought through the wind and snow, leading her directly back to the cabin. "Good girls," she said as she pushed the door opened with her shoulder, then kicked it closed again.

With fear again choking her, she lowered Jen to the floor next to the stove. She took her coat off, then struggled to remove Jen's. Her skin, although still unbearably cold, seemed to be regaining some of its color. She gently brushed the hair from Jen's face, relieved to still see movement behind her closed eyelids, relieved to hear a quiet moan.

"Can you hear me? Open your eyes, sweetheart." She patted Jen's face softly, moving her hands over her frozen cheeks. "Jen? I know you're there. Come on."

She took Jen's hands and pulled her gloves off. They were like ice cubes to the touch and she rubbed them together. She debated on whether the stove was the best option for Jen or a hot bath, but she didn't want to leave her. There was another quiet moan, then Jen's eyes opened fully.

"Jen? Stay with me."

She stood, pulling Jen up with her. Still mostly unresponsive, Jen leaned heavily against her. Ryan wrapped her arms around Jen, holding her as close as she could while continuing to rub her back. At last, she felt Jen start to shiver, and she let out a sigh of relief. Jen's body was trying to regulate her temperature. Jen finally moved, her arms snaking around Ryan's waist and holding her tightly. Ryan closed her eyes as she felt Jen bury her face against her breasts.

"I'm so sorry," Ryan said. "So sorry."

Jen's hands clenched into fists, grabbing Ryan's sweatshirt tightly. Her shoulders shook, and Ryan's heart nearly broke when she heard her begin quietly crying.

"I'm sorry—"

"No, I'm sorry," Ryan said. "I took too long. The dogs—"

"You didn't come back. I thought something happened to you."

"Jesus, I'm sorry."

"I went to look for you."

"I know. Shhh, it's okay. It's my fault. I didn't realize how long I'd been gone."

Jen lifted her head, her eyes damp with tears. "That was another idiot thing I've done," she said as she tried to smile. "I don't know what I was thinking."

"You were thinking I was in trouble," Ryan said.

Jen nodded, then buried her head again. "I couldn't see a thing," she said, her voice muffled against Ryan's chest. "I was just so worried about you."

"I'm sorry," she murmured again. "So sorry."

They stood there by the stove for long minutes, still holding tightly to each other. Ryan's hands were moving aimlessly across Jen's back as she relished the closeness. Was it inappropriate? Perhaps, but she made no move to untangle from her.

Jen finally shifted, and Ryan loosened her grip, letting Jen step away from her. Their eyes met and Jen reached for Ryan's hand, seemingly not wanting to break contact.

"Still cold?"

Jen nodded.

"How about a hot bath?"

"That would be wonderful."

"Stay here by the stove. I'll run the water."

While the tub was filling, Ryan rummaged in her drawers, finding a pair of sweatpants and shirt for Jen. She put them in the bathroom, then went back to get Jen.

She was standing by the stove, arms wrapped around herself. She turned when Ryan approached, smiling apologetically. Ryan shook her head.

"Don't you say you're sorry," she warned. "This one's on me."

"Okay. How about a cup of coffee?"

"Yes. I'll make some. Go get in the tub."

Jen left the door open to the bathroom, and Ryan's imagination went into overdrive each time she heard water splashing. She could vividly picture the scene in her mind. She busied herself with the coffee, making a tray to take out to the living room, trying to chase her thoughts away. She stood at the stove, her back to the room, staring out into the dark, stormy night. Half an hour ago she was scared for Jen's life. Now, she was picturing her naked in her bathtub.

"Thank you."

Ryan turned, seeing Jen—silhouetted by the lone lamp—dressed in Ryan's clothes. Her hair was damp and brushed away from her face. Ryan stared, thinking she'd never seen a more beautiful sight. Their eyes held for a long moment, then Ryan shook herself, motioning for Jen to join her at the stove.

"I'll bring the coffee."

They stood side by side, quietly sipping their coffee, listening to the crackle of the fire as it drowned out the raging blizzard that continued outside their cozy cabin.

\*\*\*

Jen tried to lie still, but the events of the past few hours had taxed her limitations. How close had she been to succumbing to the elements? She had no recollection of falling, no idea if she'd lost consciousness or not. She just remembered the constant fear that gripped her when she couldn't find the cabin, couldn't find Ryan and the dogs. Once again, she'd proven how inadequate she was to this lifestyle. As if driving into the path of an avalanche wasn't enough, she had to further show her shortcomings by getting lost in a blizzard. Lost...and nearly freezing to death.

"Do you want me to hold you?"

Jen closed her eyes for a moment, then opened them again to the darkness, touched by Ryan's concern. Although feeling a bit needy, she could not refuse the offer. "Yes, please."

"Roll over on your side, away from me," Ryan instructed.

Jen did as she was told, then held her breath as Ryan scooted up close behind her, folding her long body around her own. Jen reached for Ryan's hand, pulling it tightly to her. For someone who didn't like to sleep with anyone, didn't want anyone in her space, she felt totally comfortable with Ryan. She felt secure...and warm. And safe.

When she felt Ryan's soft breath on her neck, she sighed contentedly. At that moment, there was no place in the world she'd rather be. That thought, while startling, did not shock her as much as it should have.

The hand around her stomach tightened, and she ran her fingers over it, loving the softness of Ryan's skin. Her fingers trailed back and forth slowly, with only the barest of touches. Her eyes slipped closed, and she had a sudden vision of that hand moving higher, across her breasts. Her heart lurched in her chest, her pulse racing at the thought.

She acknowledged that things seemed to have changed between them. She'd felt it all day, the underlying tension that seemed to have sprung up around them. A tension that she was terrified to put a name to.

Instead, she stilled her movements and willed sleep to come.

***

When she was sure Jen was asleep, Ryan let out the breath she'd been holding and moved quietly away from her. Because it felt too good to stay where she was. She silently groaned as she stared into the darkness. It had just been too long, she reasoned. Too long since she'd been with a woman. Too long since she'd even held a woman, much less made love. She was certain that was the only reason her libido was making itself known. She just had to control it for another few weeks, at most. Then the snow would melt, the lower road could be cleared...and Jen would be out of her life.

Five weeks ago that thought would have thrilled her. Now, it brought only uncertainties and a feeling of loneliness. Which, of course, was absurd. She liked being alone. She enjoyed her solitude, her seclusion. In fact, she could hardly wait for things to get back to normal.

She closed her eyes, hoping sleep would come. Instead, she felt Jen stir and roll over. Ryan froze as Jen moved closer. One arm slipped around her waist as Jen nestled against her shoulder, her warm breath tickling Ryan's neck. She lay still, afraid to move, afraid to touch. But that need to feel someone—Jen—touching her was too much. She lifted her shirt slightly, nearly moaning as Jen's hand—even in sleep—found its way to her warm skin. It was torture but still, such a sweet torture. She relished the contact, and it was enough, just having Jen touching her. She relaxed, feeling herself drifting to sleep when Jen moved again. The hand that had been resting gently on her skin tensed, and she knew Jen was awake, knew Jen was aware of the position of her hand. Ryan waited, preparing herself for Jen's withdrawal, for her retreat. It never came. Instead, Jen's hand relaxed again, and Ryan was surprised to hear a satisfied sigh as Jen burrowed against her once more.

# CHAPTER FIFTEEN

Jen stared out the window, amazed by how much snow covered the deck. The storm had passed, leaving only flurries in its wake, and now the sun was peeking through the ever-decreasing clouds. It was nearly noon, but she'd only been out of bed a couple of hours. She felt totally wiped out and couldn't find the energy to get up and moving. Yes, that was the only reason she stayed in bed. It had nothing to do with the embarrassment she felt when she woke. Not only was her hand still tucked snugly under Ryan's shirt, she found Ryan wide awake and looking a bit amused by the whole situation. And why not? Jen had been practically lying on top of her. With as much grace as she could muster, she'd rolled off Ryan and dutifully turned her back as Ryan got out of bed. She remained under the covers, telling herself she was too warm and comfy to get up, despite the raging urge she had to visit the restroom.

Only when she heard Ryan leave with the dogs did she venture out. A scribbled note left on the bar told her not to worry, no matter how long they would be gone. They were apparently going to the ridge to check out the snow depth.

A few pieces of bacon remained on the stove and she nibbled them while she sipped her coffee, all the while trying to keep her thoughts on a neutral subject. Unfortunately, they kept returning to the scene in bed. Yes, she knew where her hand had been. Yes, she should have removed it when she'd woken up the first time. But it felt too good.

That was the problem, wasn't it? It felt too good. And she wasn't used to feeling that way.

She turned away from the window, feeling her pulse quicken. *What's happening to me?* But she shook her head. There wasn't any need to pretend, was there? Not any longer. She just didn't know what to do about it. Yes, okay, so she was attracted to Ryan. That didn't *mean* anything. She was stuck here with her; she had to rely on Ryan for everything. That was all it was. A form of the Stockholm Syndrome perhaps. Of course, she wasn't a hostage, so did that really apply? She laughed at the direction of her thoughts, thankful she could find some humor in her situation.

She turned to the door when she heard Ryan and the dogs outside. She heard Ryan knocking snow from her snowshoes. She knew the dogs would be waiting to be let inside. She knew the door would open and the dogs would run in, and she knew that Ryan would pause to stomp her boots on the mat. She knew their routine like the back of her hand.

When the door opened, the dogs burst in, running to her and bumping around her legs as they vied for attention. She petted them both equally, then shyly glanced up at Ryan.

"How do you feel?"

Jen nodded. "I'm good. Felt nice to sleep in."

They were both quiet, their glances darting around the room, landing anywhere but on each other. Jen finally motioned to the kitchen.

"Coffee?"

Ryan nodded. "Yeah. Please." Ryan followed her, leaning a hip against the counter as Jen poured coffee for them. "We had about three feet of snow," she said. "The trail was buried again. I'm amazed that the dogs could find the route, but we knocked it down pretty good."

"You went up the ridge?" Jen asked, handing a cup to Ryan. Snow still clung to Ryan's dark hair, and Jen reached up, brushing it away. Her fingers grazed Ryan's cheek and their eyes locked. Jen felt her pulse race; she couldn't pull away. There was a look in Ryan's eyes that both frightened her and excited her at the same time. She let her hand fall to her side, but their stare was only broken when Ryan lowered her gaze to Jen's mouth. Jen held her breath, so afraid Ryan was going to kiss her...and so afraid she would not.

Startled by her thoughts, shocked by the war going on inside her, she let her breath out when Ryan turned away from her, moving quietly back into the living room. Jen sighed heavily as she stared at the floor, acknowledging the disappointment she felt...and the relief.

"Jen, I'm trying to do the right thing here."

Jen looked up, glad Ryan's back was to her. She didn't pretend not to know what Ryan meant by that statement. She swallowed, nodding. "I know."

\*\*\*

Ryan felt a restlessness she hadn't felt in years. Her laptop was opened, yet her fingers remained motionless on the keys. They had no Internet and probably wouldn't for a couple of days. Jen, too, was staring at her laptop, although she appeared to be reading. Tension permeated the room, hanging so heavy between them that Ryan knew even the dogs felt it. Their intelligent eyes darted between the two of them, their quiet whimpers nearly as unsettling as the silence.

Finally, by midafternoon, the sun broke through the clouds completely. The bright sunshine bounced off the snow in waves, sending a warm cheery glow into the cabin. She stood, and both dogs jumped to attention. Jen glanced at her with raised eyebrows.

"Gonna shovel snow off the deck," she said.

Jen nodded. "I'll help."

She had to forcibly push the door open—the snow had drifted up against the cabin more than four feet. The earlier chill was fast disappearing in the sunshine, and Ryan found no need for a coat.

"It's almost balmy," Jen said as she tossed her coat back inside the cabin.

The light powdered snow of winter, this was not. It was wet and heavy, making the chore of cleaning the deck harder than normal. They both went to work with shovels, clearing the snow from the wood. She went to the railing and looked down. The lower sundeck was completely covered. She would leave that one to melt on its own. Which shouldn't be long, she reasoned. Even now, the constant drip, drip, drip of melting snow could be heard as the warm rays of sun made the ice shine like crystals. It was a beautiful sight, but she wouldn't mind the passing of winter. Green trees and bare earth, birds and chipmunks, flowers and sunshine—she longed for it all. Maybe, as Jen had said, she wasn't really such a hermit after all. She longed for the day she could drive down to Sloan's Bar for a burger and beer.

"I can't believe it's melting already," Jen said. "It's falling off the trees in clumps."

"Yeah. It's also because it's a heavier snow." She looked to the sky, seeing nothing but blue. "Evidence of this storm will probably be gone in three days. Once it stays warm, snow melts quickly," she said. "They'll probably start plowing the lower road next week."

"Yes, I know you'll be glad to get rid of me."

Ryan shook her head. "I didn't mean to indicate that you'd worn out your welcome," she said. "But I'm sure you're ready to get out of here. Get back to your life." She paused. "Where it's...safe."

Jen held her gaze with a question in her eyes. "Am I not safe here?"

The tension between them was thick again, and Ryan swallowed nervously. "Of course you are," she said. "I would never do anything—"

"I know you wouldn't. And I'll be out of your hair soon so you won't have to worry about...*doing* anything."

Jen spun on her heels and stormed off the deck, ignoring the snow they had yet to shovel. The dogs again looked between them, and Ryan motioned with her hand toward the edge of the cabin where Jen had disappeared to. Both dogs followed her instruction, leaving her alone to stew over Jen's words.

*I'll be out of your hair soon so you won't have to worry about... doing anything.*

God, what did Jen want from her? As she'd said earlier, she was trying to do the right thing. The right thing wasn't necessarily what she *wanted* to do. But anything else would be unacceptable.

***

Jen stormed around outside the cabin, sinking in the snow with each step but hardly caring. The dogs came after her, and she turned, expecting to see Ryan. She wasn't sure she was glad or disappointed that she had not followed her.

"She sent you to babysit, huh?"

She reached down, rubbing both of their heads, then let them lead her up the trail to the ridge. As Ryan had mentioned, they'd made a dent in the snow and it wasn't hard walking. She just needed to get away for a while. She was frustrated. And she was angry. She paused, considering that last thought. Angry with Ryan? Or with herself?

She blew out an exasperated breath. She wished she knew when she'd changed. It had been so subtle, she hadn't even realized it until now. Her only sexual experience was with Brad. Yet here she was, feeling more...*alive*...than she ever had. How could a look into Ryan's eyes cause her more excitement than a touch from Brad? How could her heart race from an innocent touch by Ryan, yet still beat its same steady rhythm when Brad made love to her? How could she possibly know what Ryan's kisses would be like? How could she know what her touch would feel like upon her skin? How could she want that so much? How could she want all of that so much, yet know nothing about it?

She stood, gazing out over the white landscape, letting the serenity wash over her. This would all be over soon. She could get back to her life, back to normal. These weeks would be nothing more than a fond memory, something she was sure she would take out and examine from time to time.

She would miss it here, she admitted. She would miss the views, miss the mountains. Miss their daily hikes. Miss shared meals. Miss just sitting quietly by the fire, no conversation needed.

A nudge by Kia made her glance down, seeing twin tails wagging.

"And I'll miss you too," she said. She took a deep breath, nodding slowly. "And I'll miss Ryan."

# CHAPTER SIXTEEN

The days—and nights—seemed to crawl by. The tension was there, yes. But so was the silence. It was almost as if they'd reverted back to the first week, Jen thought. There was little conversation between them and lots of time spent on their laptops. She even saw a familiar brooding look on Ryan's face, a look she hadn't seen since the first few weeks of her stay. She couldn't decide what was worse—the strained conversation during meals or the unbearable tension at night when it was time for bed. The last three nights, Ryan had made some excuse to stay up later than normal, leaving

Jen free to go to bed. Each morning, Ryan was already up when Jen woke. If there hadn't been the rumpled evidence of the bed and pillow, she would have thought Ryan hadn't come to bed at all.

The only thing even remotely normal between them was the daily hikes they took. The snow was melting fast, even though there were still deep pockets of it in shaded areas. It was nice to see the earth, see rocks and boulders, see the pines and spruce trees without snow clinging to their branches. And it was nice to see—and hear—chattering squirrels and foraging birds, hinting at springtime, a precursor to warmer days. Of course, she wouldn't be around to see those days, and that made her feel sad.

Ryan and the dogs walked ahead of her, as was the norm. She enjoyed hanging back, enjoyed watching them. She knew she was storing it in her memory bank, etching the scene in her mind.

"Look," Ryan said, pointing to the treetops. "Golden eagle."

Jen looked on in awe, watching the huge bird soar just over the trees, catching the wind currents that carried it over the mountain and away from their view. "Wow. That was beautiful."

"Yeah. I see them quite often."

And that was the extent of their conversation as they trudged on, taking one of the lower trails down to the stream. When they'd made this trip last week, the snow had still been deep, the boulders that lined the streambed covered in snow, making for a picturesque setting. Today, the boulders were bare, the warm sun having melted the snow. The stream was rushing past them, gurgling loudly as it went on its endless, timeless trek down the mountain.

They stood watching it, neither speaking. The water, the birds, the wind all joining in perfect harmony—nature's song. Jen closed her eyes, wanting to remember this day, this hike, this stream, this song. But then another sound penetrated, a sound so foreign and out of place even the birds stopped their chattering.

Snowplows.

Jen glanced at Ryan, their eyes meeting, holding. It was a sound Jen had both hoped to hear and dreaded to hear. She wondered if Ryan felt the same.

"Sounds like they're already up to the avalanche road," Ryan said.

"Where the...where the gate was?"

"Yes. They'll stop there. They won't attempt to plow the upper road for several more weeks."

Jen nodded. She knew what it all meant, of course. Once Reese let them know the road was passable, they would hike down to meet her. And she would whisk Jen away, away from the mountain, away from Ryan. Back to civilization, back to Santa Fe, back to Brad.

Back to her life.

***

The trip back to the cabin was made in silence. Not that that was unusual, but it was a different kind of silence, Ryan noted. It was filled with trepidation, dread. At least for her. She knew she should be happy. It was time. Hell, it was past time. She was tired of the tension, tired of trying to ignore her attraction to Jen, tired of avoiding any conversation that might lead to personal questions. She knew Jen was tired of it as well. But still, she wasn't *ready* for Jen to leave. More than six weeks of having her around—the place would be empty without her.

But it was time. She would e-mail Reese and Morgan, find out how soon Reese could come up the mountain to meet them. Jen would most likely drive out of her life without so much as a backward glance. A few more weeks of solitude should put things back to normal, she thought. Then maybe she could make a dent in the manuscript she'd only been toying with the past few weeks.

Yeah, it was going to be good. Get things back to normal. Everything would be just fine.

# CHAPTER SEVENTEEN

Jen volunteered to cook dinner, even though it was Ryan's turn. Ryan had taken out the last two chicken breasts to thaw earlier that morning, and she saw Jen staring into the pantry, obviously trying to decide what to make. Ryan decided to help her out.

"There's rice. And some cream of mushroom soup and cream of chicken too. And we still have some green beans."

Jen nodded. "Baked chicken and rice it is."

Ryan kicked her moccasins off and got comfortable in her recliner. The dogs were at their normal spots on the rug, and for a moment, Ryan closed her eyes and listened to Jen in the kitchen as she started on dinner. It was a sound she was sure to miss. She sighed and pulled her laptop over. As expected, there was an e-mail from Reese. They'd plowed all the way to the avalanche guard. It would be another three weeks before they plowed the upper road and before Ryan could even think of getting her Jeep out.

"I'll drive up tomorrow to get her," she read. "Let me know what time."

Ryan stared at the words for a few seconds, then began typing her reply. "Noon..." She figured it would take them two hours to hike down. She also requested a care package, potatoes and onions and more chicken. She hesitated, then before she could change her mind, she sent the e-mail on its way.

She cleared her throat, then glanced at Jen. "Got an e-mail from Reese," she said.

Jen looked at her, eyebrows raised. "What's the word?"

"She's going to pick you up tomorrow."

"Tomorrow?"

Ryan nodded, and Jen looked away quickly. There was no smile on her face. No sign of relief. Only regret. Ryan had to admit that she felt the same.

"Okay, then," Jen said. "Wow. I guess I really will be getting out of your hair."

"You haven't been in my way, Jen. You know that."

"Yes. But it's time."

Again, Ryan nodded.

Dinner was a quiet affair, neither of them making an effort at conversation. There were so many things Ryan wanted to say but didn't. Everything sounded too personal or inappropriate for their situation. The closeness that had sprung up between them needed to be tempered, she knew that. Jen had a life to get back to and an almost-fiancé. Ryan had no intention of screwing that up by taking things in a more intimate direction. She knew by the way Jen looked at her—had been looking at her for weeks—that she would not push Ryan away. But a sexual tryst would do neither of them any good. So she said nothing, just pushed her food around, much like Jen was doing.

She cleaned the kitchen while Jen went about packing her few things. There was enough food for another meal for her and she put it away for tomorrow. While Jen was in the bathroom, Ryan took the dogs out for their last short hike of the evening. The temperature had dropped to near freezing again, but stars twinkled in clear skies overhead. It should be plenty warm for their hike down tomorrow. And for her long, lonely hike back up the mountain.

When did she change? When had her almost overwhelming desire for solitude slipped away? Sure, she had the dogs, but while they were constant companions, the conversation was always one-sided. It was nice having someone to share meals with, someone to talk to, someone to sit quietly with and not say a word. And someone to hike with, someone to notice the beauty of the mountains, someone to appreciate the serenity she felt up here. Had Jen filled a void in her life she didn't even know she had?

She stopped, letting the dogs run ahead. The moon was just rising, casting an icy glow over the remaining snow. The north side of the cabin was still completely white while the south side was bare. Soon, the trail up the ridge would be snow-free and lined with wildflowers. And the meadow down below would be a lush green where the beaver pond drained. Two beautiful sights that she wished Jen could see. Maybe they could stay in touch. Maybe she'd send her pictures of the mountain in springtime. And then in summer. And maybe again in fall when the aspens turned. Maybe they could e-mail.

Or maybe Jen would leave tomorrow and they would never see each other again.

\*\*\*

Jen put another log in the stove and closed the flue a little. It hit her that this would be the last time she'd do this particular chore. She looked around the bedroom, seeing her backpack stuffed full of her clothes. She was wearing a pair of Ryan's sweatpants, one of two pairs she'd stolen from her weeks ago. The sweatshirt was embroidered with *Yale* on the front, and she wondered if perhaps it was where Ryan had gone to college. It was a little too big for her, but it had become her nighttime wear. She had half a mind to shove it in her pack when she left, hoping Ryan wouldn't miss it.

She heard the back door open and the dogs run in, both coming to find her. Their tails wagged as they circled her, holding their heads up for her to pet. Ryan stood in the doorway watching, and Jen smiled at her.

"Gonna miss these two," she said.

"They'll miss you too."

Jen nodded, feeling a lump in her throat. She turned away quickly, making a show of turning the covers back on the bed. Ryan left her alone, to her relief, and soon Jen heard her in the bathroom.

The bedroom was toasty warm, and Jen crawled under the covers for the last time. So much had changed in the last six, seven weeks—*she* had changed so much—that she hardly recognized herself. And while she never made it to the writer's workshop, she had learned a lot. Namely, that writing the next great novel probably wasn't for her, not that she still wasn't going to give it a try. She did wonder, though, how she was going to get back to her old life. Six weeks—nearly seven—wasn't all that long to be away. Would she just slip back to the old routines? Lunch with Cheryl? Dinner with Brad? Drinks with their group of friends? Would she just revert back to her old life? Would these new feelings that had awakened in her just fade away? Would Ryan be nothing more than a memory?

She stared at the ceiling, so many thoughts crowding her brain she couldn't settle on one. She stopped trying. She would have plenty of time to sort it all out later. Plenty of time.

When Ryan came in and turned out the lamp, Jen very nearly held her breath. It would be the last time they slept together, the last time she would have this closeness. While she could never find comfort with Brad, she had found it without even trying with Ryan. The covers pulled back a little and the bed shifted as Ryan lay down. They were both still, both lying on their backs. She had so much she wanted to say, but she didn't know where to start.

Finally she found her voice. "Thank you," she said quietly. "Thank you for everything. The rescue, for taking care of me. Everything."

"You're welcome."

Jen still stared at the ceiling, trying to put her thoughts into words. "I've...I've learned some things about myself up here. Good things, I think." When Ryan didn't say anything, Jen turned her head, seeing her in the shadows. "I'll miss you." She heard a soft sigh before Ryan too turned her head.

"I'll miss you too."

The words were spoken so quietly; they seemed to hang in the air. Jen nodded and turned away. She so wanted to move closer. She wanted Ryan to hold her, but she dared not voice her thoughts. Instead, she rolled to her side, away from Ryan. She was surprised at the lone tear that rolled down her cheek. She wiped it away impatiently, hating that she felt so...so *alone* at that moment.

# CHAPTER EIGHTEEN

Jen followed Ryan as she led her down the mountain. The dogs bounded ahead of them, full of energy and excitement, neither of which Jen felt. Ryan had Jen's backpack slung over her shoulders, and Jen carried her laptop. Jen's heart felt heavier with each step that took her farther from the cabin. She'd glanced over her shoulder several times, watching it fade from view.

Their hike down was as quiet as their morning had been, quieter even than the nearly silent breakfast they shared. Jen just couldn't shake the dejection that had settled over her. Even now, she knew she should be elated that she'd soon be back home, but she felt anything but that. Quite the opposite. She was saddened by the prospect of leaving, knowing somehow that she was never going to see Ryan again. That thought brought another wave of despair over her, nearly choking the breath from her.

Ryan stopped and turned, eyebrows raised. Jen gave her a weak smile.

"Do you need to rest?"

Jen shook her head, afraid to speak. Ryan seemed to study her for a moment, then nodded before pushing on. Was Ryan feeling the same emotions that Jen was? Was she dreading this goodbye as much? Why, oh why, couldn't they talk about it? Why were they both ignoring what had become so blatantly obvious?

*Maybe because you're straight and there's a man wanting to marry you?*

That thought made her nearly laugh. Her feelings lately had strongly contradicted both of those supposed facts. She hadn't even bothered to e-mail Brad to let him know she was headed home.

"Hey, come over here. Take a look."

Jen had been so lost in her thoughts that she hadn't realized Ryan had gotten off the trail. She followed her through the trees to an overlook. The sight took her breath away.

"That's Slumgullion Lake," Ryan said. "Not much snow down in the valley, is it?"

"It's beautiful," Jen said quietly, afraid to disturb the tranquility she felt at that moment.

"Yes. Very beautiful," Ryan murmured.

Jen turned, finding Ryan's gaze on her and not the view that was spread out before them. The look in Ryan's eyes caused her pulse to quicken. It always did. But it was Ryan who looked away, turning abruptly and continuing on without another word. She blew out her breath, pausing to glance down at the lake once more before following Ryan and the dogs.

Silence, again, was her companion as Ryan walked ahead of her. It was just as well. She didn't know what she would say even if Ryan did want to talk about it. The minutes ticked by, punctuated by the sounds of their footsteps. For so long, their hikes had been accompanied by the sound of snow crunching under their boots. Today, rocks and exposed twigs and limbs crunched with a completely different sound. It was almost foreign after so many weeks in the snow.

Much too soon, Ryan stopped, shrugging out of the backpack she carried for Jen. Jen looked around, spotting the one-armed gate that blocked the road just below them. Seven short weeks ago this had all been a snowy, wintery scene. She had skirted the gate, unwittingly following snowmobile tracks to climb higher up the road. Her gaze traveled the road again, higher, seeing the mounds of snow, remnants of the avalanche. Somewhere up there, buried in snow, was the SUV she had rented. Here, though, the road had been plowed, the remaining snow shoved to the side, exposing graded gravel.

"It looks completely different," she said.

"Yeah. Not a lot of snow left down here."

"I suppose I'll need to make arrangements to have my rental towed out of here."

"Reese was going to contact the rental agency, remember?"

Jen smiled. "Oh, yes. Forgot what good connections you had with the local sheriff."

Ryan picked up the backpack again and hopped across the boulders that lined the road. The snow was slushy here, and her boots landed in soft dirt. She held her hand out. Jen paused, finally taking it and letting Ryan help her down. She leaned her laptop case against her stuffed backpack. Halfway down the mountain, they'd both shed their coats.

Jen had managed to shove hers into her pack. Ryan's was tied around her waist.

"She said she'd be here at noon," Ryan said as she unwound her coat and tossed it on top of a rock. "And unlike you, she's almost always on time."

Jen glanced at her watch. They had ten minutes. *Just ten minutes. And so much to say.* She tried to find the words. She faced Ryan, offering a small smile.

"'Thank you' doesn't seem like enough," she said finally.

"You don't have to thank me."

Jen nodded. "I am going to miss...miss it up here." She paused. "Miss you."

"Yeah. I'm going to miss having you around. I'll miss our conversations."

Jen gave a short laugh. "Like I said, some hermit you are."

Ryan smiled too, her gaze never leaving Jen's. Feeling brave, Jen moved her hand, blindly reaching for Ryan's. Their fingers entwined, then Ryan tugged her closer. Jen's heart was beating loudly, blocking out all other sounds. Ryan leaned down, her lips brushing lightly across Jen's cheek. Jen's eyes slammed closed as she held her breath, waiting. Waiting for more.

"Jen..."

Jen opened her eyes, finding Ryan's. She didn't speak. She *couldn't* speak—she could barely breathe. But she took a step closer, her body now touching Ryan's. Countless seconds passed, both trying to read each other's thoughts. Then Ryan moved, her hands cupping Jen's face, her thumbs rubbing lightly across her lips.

"Please," Jen whispered. "Please kiss me."

Ryan's mouth hovered just inches from her own. She closed the distance, her hands clutching Ryan's shirt, pulling her closer. She couldn't stifle the moan—it was out before she knew it. Warm, soft lips claimed her, the kiss gentle at first, exploring. Jen welcomed it, her mouth opening, inviting Ryan inside. The moan she heard wasn't hers. She felt her knees tremble as Ryan kissed her with a hunger she never felt before. She matched it, her hands sliding up Ryan's shoulders, pulling her closer still. She groaned with a need she didn't understand when Ryan's tongue slipped past her lips.

It was a kiss, but it was a kiss like none she'd ever experienced. Was it because Ryan was a woman that it felt so different? Was that why her heart pounded and her pulse raced? Regardless, she clung to her, keeping their bodies pressed tightly together, feeling Ryan's hands moving freely across her back, then lower, cupping her hips and pulling her intimately closer.

After all of her years of longing for passion and fireworks, she found it in Ryan's kisses. She struggled to remain standing as she returned each kiss with equal fervor, relishing the arousal she'd never felt before.

She almost fell when Ryan stepped abruptly away, keeping one hand on her arm to steady her. Her eyes searched Ryan's, seeing a confusion there that matched her own—and desire she wasn't trying to hide. Then she heard it. She let out a frustrated breath and took a step away from Ryan, separating them further. The rumble of a truck's engine grew louder, and she turned, seeing a dusty white truck—Sheriff's Department written on its side—lurching up the road toward them.

"Jen?"

Jen looked back at Ryan, not knowing what to say. What could she say? She opened her mouth to speak, but no words would come. The slamming of a truck door brought reality crashing down around her.

She was leaving. Going home.

"I come bearing gifts."

Jen turned, seeing a tall, lanky woman with short hair coming toward them carrying a large backpack. She was pretty, almost handsome. Jen nearly blushed, wondering at her sudden appreciation of attractive women.

"You remembered," Ryan said with a grin.

"Yep. Morgan made lasagna yesterday too. She stuck a couple of pieces in here for you."

Jen smiled as the two women embraced quickly, then pulled apart. Ryan motioned to her.

"This is Jennifer Kincaid."

Jen took the offered hand. "It's Jen. Nice to meet you."

"Reese Daniels. Glad you survived. I imagine it was hard living with this one."

Jen glanced at Ryan, afraid to meet her eyes. "Yes. She has her moments."

"At least I didn't chop you into little pieces, did I?"

Jen smiled at that. "No." She turned to Reese. "I really appreciate you coming up here. My rented SUV is somewhere up there," she said, motioning up the snow-covered road. "I hope you were able to contact my rental agency."

"I did. I'll have it towed down once we can get to it. Don't worry about that."

She took a deep breath, turning back to Ryan. "Well, I guess this is it."

Ryan nodded. "Yeah, I guess it is. Listen, you take care of yourself."

Jen nodded. "Yes. You too." She took another deep breath, then reached down and petted each dog before getting in the truck. Reese closed the door behind her, and Jen sat there, listening to their muted conversation.

"Morgan says they'll plow up here in about three or four weeks," Reese said.

"Great. I should be able to get my Jeep out by then."

"Come down for a beer. We'll catch up."

Jen bit her lip. She would leave and get on with her life. And Ryan would do the same. She forced a smile when Reese got in beside her. Apparently, it looked forced.

"Are you okay?"

Jen swallowed. "I'm not sure," she answered truthfully.

She turned, looking out the window again. Ryan and the dogs stood there, watching. Their eyes met, probably for the very last time, and Jen felt a lump in her throat. Ryan raised her hand slowly. Jen nodded, etching that scene in her memory. She turned away from Ryan before her tears fell.

Reese said nothing as they drove away. Jen wiped at her tears, shocked by the loss she felt. It was several minutes before she felt in control enough to speak.

"The...the SUV, I've got some luggage in there. And my phone, camera," she said.

"Not a problem. If you'll leave me your address, I'll get it shipped to you. You'll need to contact your rental company, let them know we'll tow it to Gunnison."

"Okay. Thank you. I'll of course pay whatever cost there is."

"I imagine the rental place will pay for the tow."

They were quiet again, and Jen let her gaze travel across the mountains, where snow was now only visible in patches here and there. She would miss it when she returned to the dry, arid landscape of Santa Fe.

Reese was the first to break the silence. "You know Ryan likes to pretend she's some modern-day hermit, but she's really not."

"I know."

"We could have always done a helicopter rescue for you," she added.

Jen nodded. "Yes. But I was supposed to be away for a month anyway at the lodge, so..." She shrugged. Then, "Do you know why Ryan lives the way she does?"

Reese glanced at her. "What do you mean?"

"Cut off from everyone. Alone."

"Well, she's only trapped up there for a few months, really. When the road is still passable, she comes down to Lake City several times a month."

Jen asked the question she was most interested in. "Why is she alone?"

"She doesn't trust a whole lot of people."

"I know. She wouldn't tell me much about herself. In fact, she never once told me her real name." Jen paused. "I think she was hurt. I think she's running from that."

Reese shrugged. "It's not my place to go into all that. Ryan cherishes her privacy."

Jen nodded quickly, not wanting Reese to think she was prying. "I understand." She was thankful that Ryan apparently had talked to Reese and perhaps to Morgan as well. Everyone needed someone to talk to. She was also a bit hurt that Ryan had trusted them enough to share her past. She obviously had not trusted Jen.

*** 

Ryan watched until the truck was out of sight, then abruptly turned away from the empty road. The silence was deafening. She looked around, surprised by how alone she felt.

"Just us again, girls," she murmured.

She picked up the backpack Reese had brought for her and slung it over her shoulders. She would return it on her first trip down. She took a deep breath, then pushed off, heading back up the mountain. She figured it would take her at least three hours to get back to her ridge and the cabin. She just didn't realize how lonely her hike would be without Jen.

She paused, her mind—and body—wanting to relive their kisses, to dissect each and every one. She pushed her thoughts aside, though. She wasn't ready to examine them, to consider what they could possibly mean. She would save that for later. Right now, she didn't want to think. She just wanted to let it go, just as she'd let Jen go.

"Hell, she's got a boyfriend," she reminded herself. *And he wants to marry her, for God's sake.* She shook her head, pushing that thought away as well.

She concentrated on her hike, keeping her mind blank. Afternoon clouds rolled in over the mountains, blocking the sun, and the temperature dropped. She stopped to rest several times, each time marking the absence of Jen. The dogs, too, seemed to miss her; they kept looking down the mountain. Ryan found herself doing the same.

It took her three hours and fifteen minutes to hike back, but finally the cabin was in sight. Her cabin. Her home. Her sanctuary.

Jen was gone. Now things would get back to normal. She could get on with her writing. She could get back to her solitary ambling, she and the dogs wandering across the mountain at will.

Jen was gone.

# CHAPTER NINETEEN

Jen stood at the window, staring across the street at her neighbor's house, a neat adobe home just like all the other neat adobe houses on the block. Just like her own. She sighed and turned away, her thoughts going to Brad. He was angry. He was confused. She'd been back two weeks, and they'd seen each other three times, all for dinner out. And each time she'd sent him home, not inviting him inside.

"What's going on?"

"I'm just really tired."

"Come on, Jen. Every time I want to see you, you have an excuse. I missed you so much."

She had very nearly given in, her guilt weighing heavily on her. But the thought of being with him, kissing him, touching him—and him touching her—was nearly repulsive. She needed to tell him. She wasn't in love with him. She wasn't going to marry him. At least she'd figured out that much while she was away.

*Away.*

She closed her eyes, reliving again—for the thousandth time—Ryan's kisses. Each time, like now, her pulse raced at the thought. And each time, like now, she pushed those thoughts away, wishing she could forget. Forget the kiss. Forget Ryan. And each time, like now, she couldn't.

With a weary sigh, she went back to her task of making lunch. She'd invited Cheryl over. Whether it was wise or not, she needed to talk. Not necessarily about Ryan. But about Brad. Maybe she was being too hasty. Maybe she was letting what happened in the mountains cloud her feelings. She'd already spoken to Morgan, told her about the kiss, about the feelings Ryan brought out in her. That may have been a mistake; Morgan was Ryan's friend, not hers. But she'd been so out of sorts, she just needed to talk to someone. She appreciated Morgan allowing her that, but she really needed to talk it out with Cheryl. Cheryl knew her. She would know what to say to her. And she would listen.

She'd met Cheryl for lunch the second day she'd been back, and she'd very nearly blurted it all out then. Ryan. The kiss. Her feelings for Brad or lack thereof. But Cheryl had been so excited to see her, had so many things to get her caught up on that she hadn't wanted to spoil it. They chatted like the old friends they were, and she never once mentioned the turmoil she was going through. Today, however, would be different. She'd already warned Cheryl she wanted to talk.

She'd just finished putting the taco salad together when Cheryl knocked.

"Come on in," she called.

Cheryl found her in the kitchen and gave her a quick, customary hug. "Is it too early for wine?"

Jen smiled. "You know I'm not much of a wine drinker."

"I know. But you sounded like you wanted to have a serious discussion. This is more for me than you."

Jan laughed. "Maybe I should have a glass then."

Their conversation was light and easy while they ate, ranging from gossip about mutual acquaintances to the unusually warm weather they were having for late April. Cheryl was really the only close friend Jen had ever had and one of the few people she felt comfortable around. When Cheryl filled her wineglass for the second time, Jen realized how much time had already passed.

"I know you didn't invite me over to chitchat," Cheryl said. "Something's bothering you. What is it?"

Jen shoved her plate aside, as did Cheryl. "Oh, I don't even know where to start," she said.

"I'll guess it has to do with Brad."

Jen's eyebrows shot up.

"He called me. He said you've been avoiding him since you got back. Wanted to know if you'd said anything to me," Cheryl said. "As if I'd tell him anyway."

Jen smiled. "I do feel...different," she said. "And it is about Brad. Mostly."

"You can talk to me about anything, you know that."

"I know. Thank you for that." She still wasn't certain she knew where to start. She decided to share the one fact she knew to be true. "I'm not in love with him."

Cheryl's eyes widened slightly. "Okay."

Jen took her wineglass and twirled it absently between her fingers. "I haven't slept with him. Since I've been back, I mean."

"Wow. No wonder he called me."

"I've had my doubts for a while, really. That's one reason I booked the workshop in the first place," she said. "I wanted that time away, time to reflect on our relationship, to see if I really wanted to spend the rest of my life with him."

"And I guess you came to a conclusion."

"I'm not in love with him, and I don't want to have sex with him." Jen smiled. "So yeah."

"You haven't told him anything?"

"No. But surely he knows how things are between us. Surely he can tell."

Cheryl took a sip from her wine. "I'm sure he's considered the possibility," she said. "He told me you weren't the same."

Jen nodded. "I've changed. I know I have. I've changed tenfold since we first met. I mean, you know about my past. You know how I was."

"You've changed since I met you. You have much more confidence now."

"Yes. And I'm still changing."

Jen stood, going to the same window she'd stared out of earlier. She folded her hands together, wanting so badly to tell Cheryl everything. About Ryan. About the kiss. About how much she missed her. She turned back around, finding Cheryl's watchful eyes on her.

"Do you think someone could go through adolescence and into adulthood and not realize that they might be... might be gay?"

Cheryl slowly shook her head. "No. I don't think so."

"I think maybe they could. If they were sheltered. If they didn't even know about such things."

Cheryl stood too, joining her at the window. She cleared her throat before speaking.

"Are you talking about yourself?"

Jen nodded, unable to look at her.

"What's going on, Jen?"

She took a deep breath. "I kissed her. She kissed me." She looked at Cheryl. "We kissed."

"She?"

"Ryan. The woman who rescued me."

"And...she's gay?"

Jen nodded.

"I see. And that's why you think you're not in love with Brad?"

"No." She shook her head. "No. I told you I had been feeling this way about him for a while now. Ryan has nothing to do with Brad."

"What kind of a name is Ryan anyway?"

"I don't know. It may be her last name. She's a very private person."

"Okay, wait a minute," Cheryl said, holding up her hands. "You *kissed* her? Really?"

"Yes."

"What kind of a kiss?" she asked hesitantly.

"It was an 'I want to rip your clothes off' kind of kiss," she admitted. And it was. If they'd been at the cabin instead of on the side of a mountain, she was certain that was exactly what would have happened.

"I see," Cheryl said again. "And now you think you're gay? Jen, girls—women—they sometimes—"

"No, it's not like that. I spent seven weeks there. I was attracted to her. And during the course of those seven weeks, I admitted it, I acknowledged it, I accepted it. Yet we never once talked about it. Not really. There were times when I thought she was going to kiss me, but she never did. And I wanted her to."

"Then when?"

"When I was leaving. Right before the sheriff picked me up." Jen met her eyes. "For the first time in my life, there were fireworks from a kiss. I actually felt butterflies in my stomach," she said, blushing.

Cheryl pulled her into a tight hug. "Oh, Jen, I don't know what to say."

"I know. Neither do I."

Cheryl pulled away, smiling slightly. "You really think... think that you're a lesbian?"

"I don't know. I feel all mixed up. I don't know what to do."

"But you don't see yourself with Brad? Ever?"

Jen shook her head. "No. I need to tell him. Explain."

"Explain? About kissing a woman?"

"He needs to know that it's me, not him."

"No, no, no. Trust me. You do not want to tell him that. If you want to break it off with him, tell him the truth. Tell him you're not in love with him. Tell him he doesn't do it for you. Tell him you don't feel that way about him anymore. Something. But do *not* tell him it's because of another woman."

Jen smiled sadly. "Brad is a nice person. A good person. I don't want to hurt him. He deserves somebody who can love him and be what he needs. I can't do it. I wasn't ever that person. I think we both just pretended that I was."

Cheryl put an arm around her shoulder and pulled her close. "That's what you need to tell him."

Jen leaned against her. "Do you think I'm crazy?"

"No. But do you really think you're gay?"

"I felt something with her that I have never felt with Brad." She looked at Cheryl, happy to see only concern in her eyes and not disdain. "I want to feel that again."

She moved away from Cheryl, her thoughts going to Ryan, to the kisses they had shared. It had felt so wonderfully different. Ryan's mouth was so soft, so gentle, yet hungry and demanding at the same time. And her body had reacted to that. She never knew what it felt like to be sexually attracted to someone. She'd told Ryan once that she wanted more than what she had with Brad, that there must be *more*. But why Ryan? She couldn't recall another time when she felt an attraction to a woman before. Just Ryan.

She turned back to Cheryl. "Maybe I am crazy. Maybe I'm overreacting. After all, it was just a kiss." She shrugged. "It didn't mean anything."

But it was so much more than just a kiss. Their bodies had been nearly welded together, her breasts smashed against Ryan's. When Ryan cupped her hips and pulled her even closer, she felt such a jolt of arousal, something she'd never felt before in her life. And yes, it was something she wanted to feel again.

# CHAPTER TWENTY

"Finally."

After four long weeks and another major snowstorm, Ryan finally heard what she'd been waiting on. Snowplows. She'd gotten her Jeep out and had driven as far as she could—where the avalanche had buried the road. There was still a lot of snow covering it and if she remembered from last year, it would take them three or four days to clear it up to her road. She'd waited this long, she could wait a few more days.

She whistled for the dogs, and they immediately came running. She hated to admit it, but she was starved for company and conversation. Truth was, she was starved for Jen, but that was out of the question.

She had never felt as alone as she had the last four weeks. Even in the darkest hours after her name had been leaked, after the tabloid stories, she'd never felt as disconnected as she had since Jen left. She cursed herself many times for not getting her e-mail address, at least. But what good would it have done to keep in touch that way? Jen had her life. No doubt she was immersed in it again. Ryan wondered if Jen even gave her a thought anymore. No, it was best that they hadn't kept in touch. Best for both of them.

She hiked on, back to the cabin, the snow all but gone, even on the north side of the cabin. Spring came slowly up here, but she was convinced it had arrived. Birds were coming up from the lower elevations, and chipmunks were once again scurrying about, driving the dogs mad as they chased after them. Oh, sure, snow could still fall again. She'd seen flurries in June before. But it was time to clean off the sundeck, pull out the chairs and her writing table. She could envision many warm, sunny days with her laptop, maybe a cold beer or two. Yeah, summer would make it go away—her loneliness.

Things would get back to normal.

# CHAPTER TWENTY-ONE

Jen fussed with the place settings, questioning her wisdom of inviting Brad over for a nice dinner when she planned to have *the talk* with him. It just seemed wrong to break up with him over tenderloin fillets and scalloped potatoes.

It wasn't anything she was looking forward to, but she'd avoided him long enough. He surely had to know what was coming, but knowing Brad—ever the optimist—it probably never occurred to him that she was unhappy and wanted to end their relationship. Their *romantic* relationship, anyway.

Brad was the first friend she'd made in college. And while she acknowledged that she'd changed, that they'd both changed, they still had much in common. She hoped they could remain friends, but she was prepared for him to exit her life entirely if that was his choice. That would hurt. She'd been intentionally avoiding him since she'd gotten back, but there still had been many a time she wanted to call him, to tell him something, to share something she'd seen or read, to tell him about the novel she was attempting to write.

She stared at her neatly set dinner table, picturing his face, imagining how hurt he would be.

"Maybe this is a mistake," she whispered.

No. It wasn't a mistake. And she wasn't acting hastily. And it had nothing whatsoever to do with Ryan. In fact, she'd very nearly pushed all thoughts of Ryan away in the last few weeks.

*Liar!*

Regardless, it wasn't a mistake. She'd known for months—years even—that Brad was not her soul mate, was not the person she was meant to spend her life with. There had to be more than this. She *wanted* more than this.

The sound of the doorbell startled her. Brad always just knocked so when she opened the door, she was surprised to find him standing there. She smiled at him, and though he returned it, she could see by the look in his eyes that he knew exactly what the evening would entail. Her smile faded quickly.

"Come in," she said politely.

He held up a bottle of wine. "I know we don't often have wine with dinner, but I thought we might need this." He leaned closer and placed a light kiss on her cheek. "Don't look so worried. It's going to be fine."

She sighed with relief. Brad hadn't had his head stuck in the sand after all.

"Why don't you open it?" she suggested. "Dinner is all but ready."

He was as familiar with her kitchen as she was. They both enjoyed cooking, and they'd made many a meal together. She felt nostalgic as she watched him with the corkscrew. He was a handsome man, and when they'd first met in college, she often wondered why he wanted to be friends with her. She had still been in her awkward stage, hideous glasses and all. But friends they became. And eventually lovers. But as she watched him, she knew that part of their relationship had been a mistake. There had never been any passion between them, and had she been stronger and surer of herself, she wouldn't have allowed their relationship to evolve as it had. She only hoped now they could salvage a friendship out of it all.

"You know, you've only told me bits and pieces about your stay in the mountains," he said as he poured two glasses of wine. "Yet you didn't seem disappointed you missed the workshop."

"I was disappointed at first," she said. "But there wasn't anything I could do about it, and after seven weeks, well, I adjusted." She took the glass he held out to her with a smile. "Thank you. I don't know if I told you, but she was an editor. She gave me some tips on writing and was very willing to answer my many questions. I sort of feel like I did go to a workshop."

He studied her for a moment, his expression thoughtful. "You've changed," he said simply.

She nodded. "Yes."

"I think it took you being away so long and then coming back for me to notice just how much."

"I'm sorry."

"No, no. I mean that in a good way. You look very confident. When I first met you, you were scared of your own shadow. In class, you sat away from everyone else, you wouldn't look at anyone."

"I was afraid to talk to people."

He smiled and nodded. "I could tell how beautiful you were, even though you tried to hide it behind plain, outdated clothes and glasses."

She laughed. "My plain, outdated clothes and glasses were all that I knew. Remember that book I read?"

"The wallflower one? Yes. It was awful," he reminded her.

"I know. But it did get me to change my clothes. And eventually get contacts."

"That your grandmother still thinks you wear."

"Lasik? They would have considered that surgery a huge waste of money."

"Have you spoken to her lately?"

Jen shook her head. "Not since I've been back. That's horrible, I know, but we can't have a normal conversation. I can't tell her anything without her finding fault with it. And she *still* wants me to move back to Lubbock."

"And your mother?"

"No. I haven't spoken to her since...Christmas, I guess. And you know, we get along fine now, it's just that we don't have a whole lot to say to each other. I mean, she's got a new life, new husband, new kids. We just don't have much in common." She motioned him away. "We should eat," she said as she opened the oven.

"Oh, that smells good." He peeked inside. "Your famous scalloped potatoes?"

She laughed. "I spent a fortune on the tenderloins and you're more interested in my potatoes?"

"Yes. And if you're really nice, you'll send me home with leftovers."

"Don't I usually?"

"Yes, but...well," he said with a shrug.

She met his eyes briefly, noting a touch of sadness there. She felt the same. "We'll talk over dinner," she said.

He helped her carry everything to the table, and she admitted it did look—and smell—good. She smiled with pleasure as he moaned after his first bite.

"Delicious," he murmured.

"Thank you." She'd made the scalloped potatoes because it was his favorite. It was her grandmother's recipe, and even though she'd tweaked it a little to be a bit healthier, it was still delicious. So were the fillets; her knife cut through them like butter.

"Do you think we'll still cook dinner together occasionally?"

She looked up, surprised.

"Earlier when I said you'd changed—I know what that means, Jen."

She took a sip of her wine, enjoying the taste, delaying the inevitable. "I've been content," she said. "Not necessarily unhappy, but not happy either." She stared at him. "I think you've probably felt the same."

"Content, yes. Happy? Happy enough, I suppose."

"We started out as friends. For three years," she said. "I'm not really sure when it became dating. I mean, we always went to the movies together. We always shared meals. When did we start calling it dating?"

"It was after a football game. Everyone was all excited that we'd won. And I kissed you."

She laughed. "And you didn't kiss me again for *weeks*," she reminded him.

"That's because you never acknowledged the first one."

No, she hadn't. That was because she wasn't sure what it meant. Young and clueless, that was her. Even back then, his kiss brought no excitement or sexual arousal. Just like now. But she didn't want to hurt him.

"I can't keep doing this, Brad. You are one of my very best friends in the whole world, but I can't convince myself—or you—that I'm in love with you. It's not fair to you. You need to find someone who can love you like you deserve to be loved."

He nodded. "I'd be lying if I said I didn't know this day was coming. I've known it for years. I guess I just kept hoping that it would be enough."

"Is it enough for you? Don't you want that passion, that excitement that we've never had between us?"

"I know our sex life hasn't been great. I just thought—"

"That it was enough?"

"I guess I was hoping it would change. That we would find it somehow."

She smiled sadly. "Yes, I think we probably could find it. Just not with each other."

He picked up his glass, but before he took a sip, he stared at her. "I have to ask. Is there someone else?"

"No, Brad. There's no one else." And that, she knew, was the truth.

He nodded. "So where do we go from here? Do we make an announcement to the group? You know Sherry and Michael are having their annual Memorial Day party."

"You mean go to the party together and tell them we're breaking up?"

"I mean we'll go as friends. And tell them we're having a civil breakup." He grinned. "But just because we're friends, that doesn't mean I want to know about any dates you have. At least not for a while."

"I was so dreading having this talk with you. Thank you for being so understanding."

"I know you've been avoiding me. And I knew why; I just didn't want to admit it." He went back to his dinner and so did she. "You're right, you know."

"About?"

"About just being content. We were good companions and to me, that was more important than having a great sex life."

Jen laughed. "Yes. That's what they call *friends*."

# CHAPTER TWENTY-TWO

Ryan slowed as she drove into Lake City, just past Slumgullion, thankful that now, in early May, the tourists weren't yet out and about. It felt good to get out, to drive around. She glanced in the rearview mirror, smiling as Kia and Sierra hung out the opened window, their tongues flapping in the breeze. Yes, they were probably glad to get off the mountain too.

Even though it was a cool day, she parked in the shade, cracking the windows enough to allow the girls some air. She headed directly to the sheriff's office, hoping to catch

Reese. The bell above the door signaled her arrival, and she smiled, wondering how many times she'd heard Reese say she was going to take that *damn* bell down. Eloise, the office manager, greeted her with a hug, something Ryan secretly loved.

"You just missed her. Googan had a flat, and of course, he had no spare. Up on Shelf Creek Road," Eloise said.

"I'll go see if I can find Morgan then. Just tell Reese I stopped by."

"Sure will. Good to see you again, Ryan."

Of course she was barely out the door before Eloise picked up the phone. Calling Berta at the ranger station, no doubt. She'd been told early on that Eloise and Berta knew *everything* that happened in Lake City. Ryan knew there was no chance to surprise Morgan. Not in this town.

As she expected, Morgan was waiting for her when she reached the station. After a tight hug and a quick kiss on her cheek, Morgan stepped away, head tilted to the side.

"My God, you need a haircut."

Ryan laughed. "I know. I nearly took scissors to it myself."

Morgan linked arms with her. "Come on. Let's go to Stella's."

Ryan stopped. "Oh, no. Reese said she's like a hundred years old. No way am I letting her touch my hair."

"She's got a young girl working for her now. It's perfectly safe. Reese loves her."

Ryan ran her fingers through her hair, remembering how she'd had to talk herself out of shearing it off just last week. So she gave in. "Okay. I'll give her a try."

"Great. Then I'll treat you to a burger at Sloan's. We'll catch up."

"Burger and a beer," she said. "Cold draft beer."

"We can manage that." Morgan again linked their arms as they walked. "Is that one of the things you missed? Burgers and beer?"

"Yeah. And I missed you guys. A lot. This last month has been tough."

"Really? After your company left?"

"What do you mean by that?"

Morgan stopped in the front of Stella's Hair Salon. "We really liked Jen. She spent two days with us."

Ryan raised her eyebrows. "Why?"

"She got a flight out of Gunnison. I drove her up there." Morgan paused. "We talked."

"Oh? And?"

Morgan grinned. "Just...we talked." Morgan shoved her inside the door. "Let's get you a haircut."

A young girl sat at a salon chair, reading a magazine. She smiled as they came in.

"Morgan, I wasn't expecting you."

"Hi, Amber. And we're not here for me. This is my friend Ryan. And she's in desperate need of a cut as you can see. Do you have time?"

"I have twenty minutes before Mrs. Engle shows up," she said. She stood, then motioned Ryan into the chair. "Just a trim...or—"

"I usually keep it a little shorter than this," Ryan said.

Amber glanced at Morgan. "Like Reese?"

"Not that short," Ryan quickly said.

"No?" Amber combed through her hair with her fingers. "Layered?"

"I don't own a blow-dryer so nothing that requires 'fixing.' And I don't do gel."

Amber smiled. "Yes, I figured you for the natural type."

Ryan looked at Morgan. "What does that mean?"

Morgan laughed. "That you are the no-fuss lesbian type."

"Look, just start cutting and I'll tell you when to stop," Ryan said.

"You have a very handsome face. I think you'd look good with really short hair. I finally talked Reese into it." Amber glanced at Morgan. "And it fits her perfectly, doesn't it?"

"Yes. She's gotten a bit full of herself," Morgan said with a smile. "Give it a try. It'll always grow out."

Ryan looked into the mirror, hardly recognizing herself with a head full of shaggy hair. It would certainly be easier, living like she did, to have short hair. Of course, there was the upcoming trip to The Hamptons to consider. She imagined showing up at the mansion with a boyish cut. She pictured her mother's face. That sealed the deal. She gave Amber a devilish grin. "Let's do it."

She watched as five months' worth of hair fell to the floor. As it got shorter and shorter, she very nearly changed her mind. And when Amber brought out clippers and sorted through the guards, coming up with a number six to start, she nearly bolted from the chair.

"Hold still."

"It's kinda short."

"It's supposed to be."

Amber spun her around, keeping her back to the mirror as she went to work with the clippers. The buzzing sound in her ear was nerve-racking, and she locked gazes with Morgan.

"How bad is it?"

Morgan's smile was genuine. "You look gorgeous."

Ryan nearly blushed at the compliment. "It's really short, huh?"

"Yep." Morgan leaned forward. "Get Reese to tell you about the first time she cut her hair up here. We were in Gunnison because she was afraid to face Stella."

Amber laughed at that comment. Ryan had actually never met Stella but had heard stories from Reese. The mischievous look in Morgan's eyes made her curious.

"What about Reese's cut?"

"No, no. Ask her," Morgan said with a smile.

A few more passes with the clippers and Amber was finished. Ryan was about to turn to look, but she stopped her.

"Let's shampoo first."

Ryan followed her to the back, avoiding mirrors along the way. A quick shampoo and towel dry and Ryan was again sitting in Amber's chair.

"Okay. Turn around."

Feeling a bit ridiculous, Ryan slowly turned. Her eyes widened in shock as she brought a hand up to her now very short, short hair.

"Well?" Morgan asked.

Ryan ran her hands over it, loving the feel of it. "I'm not sure. Certainly different."

"It's a great style for you," Amber said. "And as you requested, no 'fixing' or gel needed."

Morgan stood. "Come on, gorgeous. Let's go get a beer."

Ryan took two twenties from her pocket and handed them to Amber. "Will that cover it?"

"Sweet. Thanks. And I'll need to see you every three weeks or so."

"I'll try to remember."

Back out in the sunshine, Ryan paused to look around. Amazing how a new haircut could make everything look brighter, shinier, new. She supposed she would get used to it in time. She wondered what Jen would think of it. She probably wouldn't recognize her.

"You look great. Quit worrying," Morgan said.

"Reese is going to tease me."

"Yes, of course. That's what big sisters do," she said easily.

It was said casually, but it made Ryan's heart swell just the same. Morgan and Reese were good for her. They kept her grounded. They kept her involved. And they loved her.

"Thanks."

Morgan seemed to understand. She smiled at her warmly. "Sure. Now what about your girls?"

"I'm parked under that big spruce. They're fine."

When they got to Sloan's Bar, Morgan opened the door for her. "You're buying, right?"

Ryan grinned. "Of course."

The bar was just as she remembered, smelling of fried food and beer. Tracy was tending bar. She smiled broadly when she spotted them.

"Ryan! Good to see you again."

Ryan accepted her hug, glad to be back among people she knew. People she called friends.

"It's great to get off the mountain," she said. "I've been dreaming about a cold draft beer."

"Love the new haircut. Looks good," she said with a smile. "Beer coming right up. Morgan?"

"Yep. I left Berta in charge."

Instead of sitting at the bar, Morgan led them to a booth. Ryan looked at her questioningly.

"I thought we could talk and catch up," Morgan explained. "Her rental got towed, by the way."

Ryan didn't pretend not to know who "her" was. But she wasn't surprised. She'd heard trucks coming and going for the last week or so, working on the road. The official start of tourist season was only a few weeks away, and that was a popular Jeep route.

"So the road is passable up past my place? That'll save me about fifteen minutes coming into town then."

"There are still some ice patches in spots, but your Jeep should be able to make it." She paused. "We shipped her things to her. From the SUV," she clarified.

"Here you are, ladies," Tracy said, carrying two frosty mugs of beer.

Ryan licked her lips, her taste buds coming to life at the sight. "Thanks." She took a sip immediately, giving Tracy a satisfied moan. "God, that's good."

"Great. Yell if you want another."

"Thanks, Tracy," Morgan said with a smile. Tracy nodded and left them.

"What?"

"What what?" Morgan asked.

"What was that little silent communication between you two?"

"I don't know what you mean."

Ryan leaned back. "Okay. I get it. What do you want to know?"

Morgan laughed. "What makes you think I don't already know?"

"So she told you?"

"What a gracious host you were? Yes."

"And?"

"And? She said you took her sledding. Reese had fun with that. You don't come across as one who likes to *play*."

Ryan ignored that comment. It was true. "And what else?"

Morgan shrugged. "Nothing." Then she grinned. "Oh. You mean the kiss? Are you talking about that?"

Ryan actually blushed, which embarrassed her further. So, Jen had felt the need to tell Morgan—a complete stranger to her—that they'd shared a kiss. Not just a kiss. A full-fledged precursor to much, much more than kissing.

"That was stupid of me," she admitted. "I hope I didn't scar her for life."

Morgan stared at her. "God, you are clueless, aren't you?"

"What are you talking about? And why did she tell you, anyway?"

"She needed to talk." Their eyes met. "She was crying. When she left you, Reese said she was crying."

Ryan swallowed the lump in her throat, looking away from Morgan. God, why was Jen crying? She should have been happy. She was getting her life back, going back to her home, back to her friends. Back to her fiancé. Her *almost* fiancé, she corrected. Why would she cry?

"I've been really...lonely since she left," Ryan admitted. She looked at Morgan again. "Why was she crying?"

Morgan shook her head slowly. "You're such a guy sometimes, I swear." She raised her hand to Tracy. "Two more," she called. "Anyway, we shipped her things to her, her luggage from the SUV. She left her address with us."

"Santa Fe?"

Morgan nodded, then leaned back as Tracy brought them another beer. "I think I'm up for that burger now." She glanced at Ryan. "You?"

"Yes. The works, with cheese. And lots of lettuce."

"Lettuce?"

"Been a while without fresh vegetables."

"I see. Extra lettuce it is."

Morgan was staring at her, and Ryan shifted uncomfortably. "What?" she finally asked.

"Your hair," Morgan said. "You look really good. It's an attractive cut for you."

Ryan blushed for the second time.

"Anyway, we really liked Jen. She was...refreshing. Very open."

Ryan nodded. "Yes, she is."

"You, however, were not."

"What was I supposed to do? Tell her who I was? By the time I was comfortable enough with her to tell her, it was too late."

"Because she's a wannabe writer?" Morgan guessed.

"Yeah. And she's proud of what she's already published, and I didn't want to ruin that for her." Morgan just shook her head and Ryan shrugged her shoulders. "What?"

"First of all, her books sell quite well," Morgan said.

"I know. I checked," Ryan admitted.

"Secondly, not a lot of writers can say they've won a Pulitzer, especially not at twenty-two like you did. I think she would have been ecstatic to know that about you."

"You don't understand. She was so enthused about her writing, about her plans that I didn't want to embarrass her."

"Why would that embarrass her?"

Ryan stared into her mug of beer, wondering if that was just her excuse for not telling Jen or if she really thought that about her. No, Jen wouldn't have been embarrassed. She would have just asked a hundred more questions than she already had. Ryan could picture her curled up on the sofa, coffee cup in one hand while the other waved about as questions flew from her lips. No, that wasn't why she didn't tell her.

"I was afraid," she admitted to Morgan.

"That she would remember the story? That she would doubt you?"

Ryan nodded. "I didn't want her to think I was a fraud."

Morgan studied her for a moment, then leaned back. "Why did you kiss her?"

"Jesus, are you trying to get it all out before Reese finds us?"

Morgan smiled. "Yes. So why?"

"It just kinda happened."

"That's all you're going to say? It just kinda happened?"

Ryan remembered the weeks leading up to Jen's departure, fighting the attraction she didn't want, didn't need. And the surprise she felt when she realized Jen was fighting it too. Although she wasn't quite certain Jen understood it. Maybe on a more subconscious level, perhaps, but on the surface, she could see the confusion Jen felt. She cared for Jen enough, respected her enough that she didn't want to do anything to screw up her life. They both knew Jen would be leaving eventually. It wasn't like an affair would have accomplished anything other than to bring chaos into Jen's life. She didn't want to be the cause of that.

But that day, when Jen was leaving, when Jen had taken her hand, she simply couldn't resist any longer. All the weeks of wanting, of dreaming, had taken its toll. Even then, she still wasn't sure what Jen's reaction would be. Would she pull away in shock? Would she slap her? Would she be angry?

*"Please kiss me."*

No. She opened to her, like Ryan had dreamed she would. And it was too much to resist. If Reese had been even ten minutes later, there's no telling how far they would have taken it. And that thought, to this day, caused her body to yearn for something she couldn't have.

She glanced up at Morgan, not feeling the need to share her thoughts. She shrugged again. "It just happened."

Morgan stared at her for a long moment, then nodded. "Okay."

Ryan grinned. "Thanks."

"Oh, sure. Anytime."

Ryan laughed. "You're a wonderful therapist."

"Yes, I know. Thank you."

"There you two are. I should have known—what the hell did you do to your hair?"

They both turned at the sound of Reese's voice. Ryan watched with envy as Morgan and Reese looked at each other, matching smiles on their faces. She'd never seen two people more in love.

"I wondered how long it would take you to find us," Morgan said.

"I got a tip from Eloise." Reese stood, staring at her. "Your hair?"

Ryan ran a hand over her now very short hair. "We look like twins now, huh?"

Reese finally sat down. "I imagine Amber got a hold of you. She cuts mine shorter every time I go."

"Yeah, but I hear you used to get it cut in Gunnison."

"I was afraid of Stella."

"Morgan said I should ask you about the first time you got it cut." Ryan laughed as the normally unflappable Reese Daniels actually blushed. "Wow, this has got to be good."

Reese glanced at Morgan with a smile. "I think that I was the victim in that instance."

"Victim? You weren't acting like the victim at the time, sweetheart. In fact, you were nearly begging—"

"Okay, okay. She doesn't need to know all that," Reese said quickly.

"You had sex in the salon?" Ryan guessed.

Reese shook her head. "No. But while we were driving to the grocery store, she attacked me in the truck."

"Attacked? I was the one driving," Morgan said.

"Exactly. It's a wonder we didn't have a wreck, what with you shoving your hand down my pants and all."

Ryan laughed with them, again envious of their relationship. It made her wish—hope—that someday she might have that. The closeness that comes with living with someone, sharing thoughts, feelings. Laughing, playing... and loving. She wasn't all that surprised to find herself picturing Jen's face at that moment.

"So, are you down just for the day or are you staying?" Reese asked.

"I thought I'd stay the night, if you don't mind," she said. "I need to make a run into Gunnison for supplies. Thought I'd do that in the morning."

"Sounds great. Good excuse to get the grill out. I'd love a steak," Reese said.

"Are you staying for lunch?" Morgan asked her.

"No. I need to play sheriff. Googan's got his car over at Sammy's shop. Flat and no spare, so I'm taking his patrol," she explained. "You two have fun. I'll see you tonight."

"Be careful," Morgan said.

"Always."

Morgan had a smile on her face even after Reese was out of sight. "I love that woman," she said simply.

"I know."

Before she could say more, Tracy brought their burgers over. Ryan's mouth watered at the sight.

"Another beer?"

"No thanks, Tracy. But a glass of water would be great," she said as she reached for her prize. She moaned as she took her first bite. It was sinfully delicious. She had nearly devoured half of hers before Morgan even got started.

"That good, huh?"

"Excellent," she managed around another bite.

"So what are your plans for the summer?" Morgan asked. "Will we get to see you more often?"

"I imagine so. My writing's kinda stalled at the moment."

"Stalled? Why?"

Ryan shrugged. "It happens. It's the weather," she said. "I'd rather be out exploring."

"Well, it's not like you have a deadline."

"That's true," she said with a grin. "I will have to make a trip out East though. My grandmother's annual birthday bash."

"You're going again? When you came back last year, you said that was your last one."

"Yeah. I say that every year. But she's eighty-nine, and she would be terribly hurt if I didn't go. Besides, it's for a good cause."

"You hate charity events," Morgan reminded her.

"I hate charity events that involve my mother," Ryan corrected. "I will admit she's good at it and puts on a good show but that's all it is to her—a show."

"It's for Parkinson's, right?"

"Yes. My great-grandfather had the disease."

"So how many years will this be?"

"I think my grandmother was in her forties when she started having these. It's evolved over the years, and it attracts a lot of celebrities now," Ryan said with a roll of her eyes. "My mother's doing."

"I can see how much you love it," Morgan said with a laugh.

"I dread it," Ryan said. "And if it were anyone other than my grandmother, I wouldn't hesitate to say no."

"I guess it's good you're going. Maybe one of these visits, you and your mother can reconcile your differences."

"So when I tell you how shallow and superficial she is, you don't believe me?"

"Yes. I know she comes across as posturing, even on TV, but she's still your mother. There has to be some connection between you two."

"No, there isn't. We have nothing in common. My beliefs are so different than hers. Whatever ambition I had as a child, she tried to curb it. She wanted me to be a replica of her, nothing more than a wealthy woman from a wealthy family marrying into an even wealthier family. That's what her mother did, that's what she did. I was supposed to continue the cycle."

"Your parents, do they have a relationship?"

"You mean, did they marry for love?" Ryan shook her head. "No. That's not how it works. My father has a mistress."

"Does your mother know?"

"Of course. And she has her own affairs from time to time. But in public, they come across as a happily married couple. Years of practice, something they learned from their own parents, I'm sure."

"Do you think that if all of that hadn't happened with your book, you would have fallen into the same trap?"

Ryan shook her head. "No. I obviously wasn't going to marry, and my mother finally accepted that I wasn't just going through a gay 'phase,'" she said. "She turned her focus to my brother, but he has no intention of settling down. He also has no interest in delving into the family business. Nor do I," she added.

"*Is* there a family business? I mean, I know all of the hotels and everything and then the casino, but is that something that your father really has a hand in?"

"President is his official title, not CEO. But it's still a private company, so he has a lot of power. Actually, my grandmother was still involved with it too, well into her seventies."

"It's hard for me to think of you living in that world," Morgan said.

"I know. And for the last ten years, I haven't been a part of it. I could never go back."

She knew that to be true. Going back once a year, to honor her grandmother, was as much as she could stand. Once her grandmother was gone, she wondered if she'd ever go back at all.

# CHAPTER TWENTY-THREE

"So Brad's not the only guy you've slept with, is he?"

Jen felt herself blushing from head to toe at Cheryl's question. She glanced around the bar, hoping no one had heard.

"Oh my God," Cheryl said. "Seriously? That's not normal."

"Normal for whom?" Jen asked. "It was perfectly normal for me, considering I didn't know a thing about dating—or guys—until I was a senior in college."

Cheryl leaned forward. "So maybe that's the problem. He's the only one you've been with. Maybe you don't have anything to compare it to."

"What are you saying?"

"Maybe you need to, you know, date and stuff."

Jen shook her head. "No. That thought is nauseating."

Cheryl grinned. "The guy part? So then date women."

Jen laughed. "Okay, that's only slightly less nauseating. The idea of me going out and dating guys—or women— well, it's frightening. You know, that's just so out of my element. I'm not at all comfortable in that scene."

"You write self-help books, for God's sake. Do you not read what you write?"

Jen laughed again. "I don't think I've ever touched on this particular situation. Besides, honestly, I hate yoga. And I can't meditate worth a damn."

"What? But every book—"

"I know, I know," she said. "Yoga bores me. I've gone to hundreds of classes and I just don't get it. I can do the poses, the exercises, but it doesn't *move* me. I just can't connect with it like most do." She paused. "You know Susan wants me to start on a fourth, don't you?"

"Yes. Are you still stalling?"

Jen nodded. "The desire is just not there. I don't know how some put out six, seven, even ten self-help books. What can they possibly still have to say?"

"But motivational books still sell," Cheryl said.

"Oh, I know. And I'm very thankful for that. But I just don't think I can do another."

"So you're still going to try your hand at fiction?"

"I have a couple of ideas, and I have the time and resources," she said with a shrug. "If I don't do it now, when will I?"

"I just know how critical you are of your work. I don't want you to get discouraged."

Jen smiled. Yes, Cheryl knew her well. "I'll try my best not to be my worst critic."

Cheryl leaned back, watching her. "So how are you? I mean...you know."

Jen stared down into what was left of her drink. "I miss her." She looked up. "I miss her a lot." She tried to smile but failed. "I thought I'd be over it by now. It's been nearly two months. But I...I still miss her."

"Have you told Brad anything about her?"

Jen shook her head. "No. But Brad's been great. We've been able to transition into just a friendship so easily, I think he now realizes how forced our relationship was. For both of us."

"Is he dating?"

"Haven't you heard? He's been going out with Michael's sister."

"The one that was at their party?"

"Yes. Tara. She's younger, just out of college, but I think he really likes her."

"And you're okay with that?"

"Yes. I want him to be happy. We're in a good place now. We see each other at least once a week, talk on the phone more." And it was good. Their friendship had strengthened, and if she ever felt the need to talk about Ryan and her feelings—she felt certain he would listen.

Cheryl leaned forward, her voice low. "So when I start looking for someone to set you up with, should I look for a male or female?"

Jen laughed good-naturedly. "Are you asking me which gender is in my nighttime fantasies?"

"Do I dare?"

Jen looked away, remembering the very vivid dreams she had been having, dreams of touching, of kissing. Passionate dreams of making love. In each one, her fantasy lover was always Ryan. She looked up, knowing she wouldn't have to answer the question.

Cheryl nodded. "I see."

"I'm sorry if that shocks you or disappoints you in some way," Jen said.

Cheryl reached across the table and took her hand. "You could never disappoint me. But I will admit, I'm still a little shocked by the whole thing."

Jen smiled affectionately at her friend. "Thank you. And to be honest, I'm a little shocked by it as well."

# CHAPTER TWENTY-FOUR

Ryan slung her backpack over her shoulder and headed across the tarmac to her father's private jet. As was usually the case, she was dreading going back East. Dreading dealing with her mother, dreading trying to hide from the media who would be at her grandmother's birthday bash. While it would be good to see her brother, she usually could only tolerate him for a day before she wanted to run away screaming. He had not a care in the world and about the same amount of ambition as well.

As she neared the jet, a man came around the side. It was Jeffery, her father's pilot. He stopped short, staring at her for a long moment.

"Why, Miss Catherine, I hardly recognized you."

Ryan frowned, then remembered her hair. She was used to it now and was no longer startled when she looked in the mirror. She brought up a hand to rub over it, having just visited Amber for the second time two days ago.

"Needed a change, Jeffery. How are you?"

"Good. I got your message yesterday. You want to stop over for just the one night?"

She hesitated, wondering at the wisdom of her decision. She could always change her mind. In fact, that would be best. Just head straight to The Hamptons and leave well enough alone. But she couldn't.

"Yes. Just the one night."

"Okay. She's all ready to go when you are."

She nodded, then preceded him up the steps and into the plush interior of the jet, tossing her backpack on one of the seats before settling down herself. She was suddenly very nervous, and it had nothing to do with flying.

# CHAPTER TWENTY-FIVE

The afternoon sun was sinking lower, the light having moved from her window. Jen looked up from her desk, noting the colors as they changed. It appeared they would be graced with another spectacular sunset. She saved what she'd been working on—had been working on all day—and stood, stretching her back as she raised her arms up over her head.

Sunsets were something she never paid much attention to before. But during the seven weeks she'd been up in the mountains, they'd witnessed quite a few. Lately, as she'd watch the sun disappear, she often wondered if Ryan was watching too. She imagined her up on the ridge, both dogs by her side as she gazed to the west.

She couldn't believe how hard it was to push Ryan away, out of her thoughts. She seemed to constantly be there. Sometimes, she took comfort in that. Other times, like now, it just made her feel very alone. She turned away from the setting sun, as if doing that might banish Ryan from her thoughts.

She still didn't know what she was going to do. While she and Brad remained friends, he had moved on from their relationship. She wanted to as well, but she didn't know where to move *to*. The thought of dating—even though she wasn't the same shy girl she'd been in college—was daunting. And even if she did feel confident enough, the thought of meeting new people, whether male or female, just wasn't appealing to her. She told herself she wanted to focus on her writing, but maybe that was just an excuse.

Oh, she still went out with their group of friends, she still met Cheryl for lunch or dinner. And she and Brad still shared a meal at least once a week. She wasn't starved for company. She just missed the intimacy that came with being lovers. She laughed slightly as she made her way to the kitchen. While she and Brad had been lovers, their conversations had never been intimate. In fact, nothing had changed in that regard.

She opened the fridge, hoping to miraculously find dinner. The chicken parmesan she and Brad had made two nights ago was still there, but that didn't appeal to her. She closed the fridge and opened the freezer. After scanning the contents, she closed that as well. The doorbell rang just as she was about to open the pantry. She glanced at the clock, wondering who it could be.

She was still mulling over dinner options as she opened the door. She gasped in shock. Ryan looked different with short hair—more attractive, if that was even possible—

although she would have recognized her anywhere. She couldn't believe the woman who had been haunting her dreams for so many months was now standing before her, in the flesh. She couldn't find her voice, though, and she simply stared, afraid her legs were going to buckle at any moment. Ryan was the first to speak.

"I missed you."

Jen finally let her breath out. "Are you real? Or am I dreaming?"

"I'm real. Or maybe we're both dreaming."

Jen smiled. "I missed you too."

"I know I shouldn't be here," Ryan said as she glanced behind Jen into the room. "You probably—"

"I'm alone. Come in."

Jen stepped back, motioning for Ryan to enter. She saw Ryan swallow nervously and that brought a small smile to her face. When she closed the door, they stood facing each other, gazes coming together and then moving away again.

"How have you been?"

Jen shrugged. *Miserable.* But, "Okay, I guess." She reached out a hand, brushing her fingers through Ryan's hair. "I love your hair like this."

Ryan's eyes closed. Jen was shocked by the obvious power she had over her. She let her fingers continue their exploration, encouraged by the rapid pulse beating in Ryan's throat.

"Jen, we should talk—"

"No."

Whatever excuse Ryan wanted to make, she didn't want to hear it. It had been too long. There was only one possible reason Ryan was here. Feeling as brave as she'd ever felt in her entire life, she took Ryan's hand and led her through the house. Her pulse was pounding loudly, threatening to choke the breath from her, but she didn't let go of Ryan.

She pushed open her bedroom door, then turned to face her. Ryan's eyes searched hers. Jen didn't know what to say, didn't know *how* to say what she wanted. But she knew what she wanted, that she was sure of.

She finally dropped Ryan's hand as her own reached for the hem of her shirt. She took a deep breath, then slowly pulled her shirt over her head. Ryan's gaze traveled over her bare torso, landing on the red lacy material that still covered her breasts. Fueled by the clear desire on Ryan's face, Jen reached behind her and unclasped her bra, letting it fall away. She watched Ryan's chest rise and fall, saw her tongue come out to wet her lips. She felt a thrill as Ryan's hungry gaze traveled over her. She stood still, a silent offering.

"My God, you're beautiful," Ryan whispered. Then she raised her eyes, "Jen, you don't—"

"Don't speak," she said softly, placing a finger across her lips. "Don't think. Just feel. Just...*do*."

Ryan nodded as her gaze returned to Jen's breasts. "I want to make love to you."

Jen smiled. "I was kinda hoping you did, seeing as I'm half naked."

Ryan quickly shed her own shirt, then hesitated only a second before taking her bra off as well. Jen's eyes were drawn to her; she was as beautiful as Jen had imagined. She looked up, meeting Ryan's gaze, seeing her desire mirrored back at her. Weeks—months—of dreaming of this and Ryan was here, she was real. She was no longer only a fantasy lover. Jen smiled shyly, not knowing what to do.

Ryan smiled too, taking a step toward her. Jen felt her heart jump in her throat. She swallowed her nervousness. Ryan's first touch sent chills across her body, and she nearly moaned from it.

"If you want me to stop, just say—"

"I want you to stop talking, that's what I want," Jen murmured as she found Ryan's mouth, effectively silencing her.

The kiss was the same as before, yet oh so different. Jen didn't hesitate, her mouth opening, her tongue battling

Ryan's as if she'd done it many times before. Soft lips seemed to devour her and she gasped as Ryan's hands moved up, cupping her breasts. She moaned into Ryan's mouth as fingers rubbed across her nipples, the sensitive buds turning rock hard from Ryan's touch. She pulled her mouth away, needing to breathe, and she gulped in deep breaths. Yes, she had dreamed of Ryan touching her, yet she wasn't prepared for the way her body reacted. She felt her knees weaken, afraid she would collapse right there when Ryan's fingers slipped to her waist, deftly unbuttoning her shorts in one quick motion. It was all a blur. Ryan's hands seemed to be everywhere at once. Jen's senses were on overload. She found herself completely naked and on the bed, reaching for an equally naked Ryan and pulling her down to her.

When Ryan's body covered hers, she was amazed at the smooth softness of her skin. As her hands traveled across Ryan's back, Ryan nudged her thighs apart. Jen's hips instinctively shifted, rising up to meet Ryan's body as she pressed into her.

"It feels so good," she murmured. "I've been dreaming of this."

"You have no idea," Ryan whispered against her lips.

The hand that moved down her body was slow and sure, and Jen trembled as Ryan slipped it between her thighs. She could feel her own wetness, and she spread her legs, urging Ryan to take her.

She gasped as Ryan's fingers moved through her slick folds, her hips jerking when those fingers rubbed across her clit. She had never been more aroused, had never wanted like this before. She pulled Ryan's mouth to hers, moaning when Ryan sucked her tongue inside the same instant as her fingers filled her.

Jen didn't know what she expected, but the sheer bliss of it all was nearly too much for her to stand. She pulled her mouth away, breathing deeply, her hips moving against Ryan in a natural rhythm. Ryan lowered her head, her tongue raking across her nipples, first one then the other. Jen moaned again as Ryan covered her breast, sucking a nipple into her mouth. It was all too much—too much, too soon—and her body simply exploded, bursting from pure pleasure. She hardly recognized the scream that came from her mouth, but she couldn't possibly have kept it in.

Before she had time to register the magnitude of her orgasm, Ryan moved down her body, both hands spreading her thighs apart. Jen looked down, her eyes wide.

"What...I can't...I've never...oh, dear *God*," she breathed when Ryan's mouth settled over her clit, sucking it hard, rubbing her tongue against it. Jen's hands clutched the sheets, her hips rocking wildly against Ryan's face. The feeling was so wholly different than anything she'd experienced; she wanted it to last forever. Her body, however, wouldn't cooperate. She felt her world spinning out of control, and her second orgasm hit with nearly the same force as the first, taking her breath away as she squeezed Ryan's head between her legs.

Her legs and arms fell limply to her sides, her eyes closed, her mouth open, drawing quick breaths. Ryan's hands moved slowly now, softly caressing her body, as she whispered words Jen couldn't decipher.

"Incredible," Jen whispered. "Absolutely incredible."

"Was that your first time?" Ryan guessed.

Jen nodded. "I've never felt this way before."

"I'm glad."

Jen rolled to her side, facing Ryan. "I can't believe you're here." She smiled. "I can't believe you're in my bed and...and we just..." She stopped, her gaze drawn to Ryan's mouth. "Show me. Teach me. I want to please you. I want to make you feel this way." She leaned closer, softly kissing Ryan on her lips, tasting herself as she did so. "Please...show me what to do."

Ryan took her hand and slowly moved it between their bodies. Jen waited in anticipation as Ryan's thighs parted.

"Oh God...you're so..."

Ryan smiled against her lips. "Wet."

"Yes," Jen whispered.

Ryan moved her hand again, sliding it between Jen's own legs this time. "Just like you are."

Jen felt her wetness with her own fingers, shocked at how aroused she still was. Ryan moved their hands, brushing against Jen's clit. She jerked, a thrill passing through her. "*God*," she moaned, then, "*No*. No, no, no." She rolled them over, straddling Ryan's hips.

Ryan pressed up into her, a slight smile on her face. "No, no, no?"

Jen stared at her, surprised at how confident she felt at that moment. The insecurities she normally harbored—with Brad—vanished with Ryan. She now understood why sex with Brad had always left her wanting more. She just had no idea that *more* involved a woman. She lowered herself, kissing Ryan passionately.

"I want to know you. All of you." She shifted, her hand moving tentatively to Ryan's breast, amazed at the softness she felt. Ryan moaned when Jen's fingers brushed her nipple. It became rigid and Jen was drawn to it; her mouth—timid at first—finally closed over it, her tongue circling the hard peak.

Ryan pulled her closer, emitting sounds of pleasure, her hands roaming her back at will, all making Jen more aroused than she already was. Ryan spread her legs and Jen settled between them, her hips unconsciously rolling against her. She lifted her head from Ryan's breast, her lips finding Ryan's again.

"Are you going to show me what to do?" she whispered.

Ryan smiled against her mouth. "What you're doing now is pretty fantastic."

Jen pulled back, smiling too. She couldn't believe how at ease she felt, how comfortable she was with Ryan. It seemed the most natural thing in the world for her hands to move down Ryan's body, fingertips brushing across smooth skin. With a confidence she didn't know she had, she nudged Ryan's legs apart, her fingers going to where she had only dreamed of, finding the wet warmth she sought. She moaned when she first touched her—like silk on her fingers—and her eyes found Ryan's as she slipped inside her. Ryan's hips rose up to meet her, opening for her.

"Yes," Ryan murmured. "Like that."

It was slow and sensual, her fingers buried inside Ryan, thrusting a little faster now as Ryan set the pace she needed. Jen tried to take it all in, but it was sensory overload. She lowered her head, her mouth closing over a rigid nipple, moaning as she suckled it. Ryan's hand in her hair held her mouth there, and Jen was happy to comply.

Ryan's free hand slipped between Jen's thighs, seeking—finding—her clit. Jen gasped as she pressed into Ryan, her hips undulating, surging to meet Ryan's strokes.

"Yes, harder," Ryan breathed, her own hips bucking against Jen.

Jen tried desperately to keep pace. It was the most erotic thing she had ever done, and she lifted her mouth from Ryan's breast, needing desperately to breathe. Their hips rocked together, their hands between their bodies, each pleasuring the other. Jen locked gazes with Ryan, awed by the sheer ecstasy she felt at that moment. She thrust harder, her breath coming as fast as Ryan's, matching Ryan stroke for stroke.

Wanting to hold on, to make it last, she couldn't. The pleasure was too much. Her breath caught, her hips jerked one last time.

"Yes...*now*," Ryan urged, her own hips suspended in air as her thighs clamped down on Jen's hand. She groaned loudly, and Jen gave in too, her orgasm washing over her in waves of sheer bliss.

She collapsed on top of Ryan, totally spent. Their skin was damp with perspiration, and she felt Ryan's fingers brush the hair from her face. She tried to move but simply didn't have the energy.

"Are you okay?"

"Fabulous," Jen managed before closing her eyes completely.

# CHAPTER TWENTY-SIX

Ryan's eyes fluttered open, then closed again. Jen was snuggled against her, still sound asleep. She finally forced her eyes open, the events of the night registering. The corner lamp was still on. Ryan watched Jen, her features relaxed in sleep. She had never seen anything more beautiful.

Panic set in. *What have I done?*

She untangled herself slowly from Jen, quietly getting out of bed. Jen stirred but didn't wake. She stared at her, memorizing the curve of her face, the slope of her nose, her lips, her eyes, her mouth. God, that mouth had been everywhere on her body, it seemed. She closed her eyes for a second, taking it all in.

"I'm so sorry," she whispered.

She took a deep breath, then turned, picking up her discarded clothing and slipping from the room. She dressed quickly, trying not to think about what they'd done—what she'd done. She just needed to escape.

At Jen's desk, she took a piece of paper from a notepad, pausing when she spotted Jen's laptop. She ran her fingers across it, remembering many an evening with Jen curled on her sofa, typing away. Ryan shook the memory away as she grabbed a pen. She stared at the paper, not knowing what to say. She finally scribbled an apology and fled.

The sun was not up yet, and only then did Ryan think to look at her watch. Four thirty. She jogged to her rental car, pausing to look back at Jen's house once before speeding away.

She didn't understand her need to escape, but it was strong and she went with it. She sped down the unfamiliar streets, back to the highway.

"What the hell have I done?"

They hadn't talked. Not really. It was like they couldn't stop touching, couldn't stop kissing long enough to talk. She never once asked about Brad, and Jen didn't mention him. Hell, for all she knew, they were engaged by now. They might even have set a wedding date. She felt panic setting in again and pushed those thoughts away. She pounded the steering wheel with her right hand, cursing herself for what happened. But really, wasn't that exactly what she'd hoped would happen? Why else had she shown up on her doorstep? She'd been thinking about Jen day and night, since the moment she walked out of her life. She just needed to get her out of her system, she told herself. And after spending hours in bed with her, surely to God she had.

But what about Jen?

She slowed, glancing in the rearview mirror. She should go back. She couldn't just walk out on Jen like that. She met her gaze in the mirror and shook her head. No. She couldn't go back. She sped up again, moving farther away from Jen with every second.

She couldn't go back.

***

Jen rolled over, stretching her legs out. She was pleasantly sore. A sudden smile lit her face. It faded quickly, though. She knew even before she opened her eyes that she was alone. She reached over, feeling the coolness of the sheets. The house was quiet. Too quiet.

Ryan was gone.

She stared at the ceiling, feeling an ache in her chest. *Ryan was gone.* She forced herself out of bed, seeing her bra on the floor, her shirt and shorts, and she was very aware of her own nakedness. "We made love," she whispered, steadying herself at the edge of the bed. "I made love with her." Yes. And she felt incredibly alive. And Ryan was gone.

She took her robe, covering herself with it before walking slowly through the house. She saw the note and stopped, swallowing down the lump in her throat. Her hand was trembling as she picked it up.

*"I'm so sorry, Jen. Please don't hate me."*

She clutched the note in her fist, holding it to her heart. "Oh, Ryan, what are you running from?"

# CHAPTER TWENTY-SEVEN

Ryan stood looking at the mansion, her backpack slung casually over one shoulder. The ocean breeze brought a pleasant scent in, one very different from the mountain air she was used to breathing. Still rooted to the spot, she wasn't prepared to see her mother. Normally, she used the long flight to steel herself for the three days she'd be here, toughening her skin so her mother's words would bounce off of her. Today, however, all she could think about was Jen...and the way she'd snuck out of her bed, out of her house. Out of her life.

It was for the best, she told herself. Damage control. This way, Jen didn't have to face her, didn't have to face the fact that they'd had sex. This way, Jen could just get on with her life. She didn't need the complications that Ryan would bring to it.

Ryan finally made herself move. The mansion looked as it always did. Huge and intimidating. It was hard to call it home. She was greeted at the door by Arthur. She smiled at him. He'd worked for her family since she was a child.

"Miss Catherine. I daresay I hardly recognized you."

"Good. Maybe my mother won't either," she said as she ran her hand over her short hair.

He leaned closer, his voice quiet. "This may give her that stroke you've been hoping for."

She laughed. "I was thirteen when I first said that. You wanted Maria to wash my mouth out with soap," she reminded him.

"So I did." He stepped back, welcoming her inside. "How have you been?"

She paused. "Good," she said. "Anything new here I should know about?"

"Your mother is busy with the caterers at the moment. I believe she was expecting you yesterday," he said.

"Yeah. I had to make a detour," she said vaguely. "So I have a reprieve?"

Arthur smiled. "I believe you could hide from her until dinner, yes. Shall I take your bag to your room?"

"I can manage," she said.

"Very well. I shall ask Sophie to bring you up a late lunch. I don't imagine you've eaten."

It was only then that she realized how hungry she was. Ravenous, really. "Thank you. That would be great."

He bowed, as was his custom, and she headed for the staircase, her gaze following its twisting curve up to the second floor. With a weary sigh she walked up, trying to conjure up some happy memories of the place. As usual, she couldn't. She would always remember the mansion as the place she fled from ten years ago.

Her room was large and airy, with two windows facing the ocean. She tossed her bag on the bed and immediately opened the double doors, walking out to the terrace. She breathed in the scent of the sea air as her eyes were drawn to the waves crashing on shore. She remembered many a night when she would sneak down there, sitting for hours just listening to the surf, writing stories in her head, afraid to let anyone know of her passion.

A light tap on her door signaled Sophie's arrival. She went back inside and opened the door, smiling politely at the young woman who had taken Maria's place several years ago.

"Miss Catherine, good to see you again."

"Thank you, Sophie." She lifted the lid on the silver serving tray, finding perfectly cut sandwich wedges, along with cucumber slices and cherry tomatoes. Her stomach growled. "Very nice."

"Please ring if you need something else," Sophie offered.

"This should be fine."

There appeared to be three different sandwiches. Ryan grabbed the roast beef first, moaning at the first bite. She piled a plate high, then grabbed the bottle of water Sophie had supplied and went back out to the terrace. As she finished off the roast beef and started on the turkey, she paused, her thoughts going back to Jen. Was she wrong to have left like she did? Should she have hung around long enough to make sure Jen was okay? What would she have said?

"*I'm on my way to The Hamptons and thought I'd stop by and screw up your life.*"

She shook her head slowly. God, what was she thinking by stopping by in the first place? If it was just sex she wanted, she could have gotten that anywhere. She would see many willing women in the next few days. Most of them just like Megan had been, willing to do anything to be a part of the Ryan-Barrett clan.

Maybe that's why Jen had such a hold on her. She was not like Megan. She was *real*. Their lovemaking had been *real*. It was a night Ryan knew she would never forget. Jen's touch, so innocent and tentative at first, had grown bolder and surer, leaving Ryan transfixed and wanting more. And Jen gave her more...for hours and hours, she gave her more.

Ryan blew out a breath, hating herself at that moment. She shouldn't have left. She should have stayed. They should have talked. She should have explained. Explained that she couldn't offer Jen anything other than what they'd just shared.

Sex.

Yes, that's all she ever could offer. Just sex. Nothing more. But Jen deserved so much more than that.

Her appetite vanished suddenly. She went back inside, placing the uneaten food back under the tray. The restlessness she normally felt here hit her then, and she left her room, needing a diversion from her thoughts.

She went up to the third floor where her grandmother's rooms were. Abby, who had been with her grandmother for years, greeted her.

"Miss Catherine, you've come. She's been asking for you."

Ryan looked past her into the room. "Is she up?"

"I just woke her from her nap, yes. I was about to make her a cup of tea. Would you like one too?"

"Coffee?" Ryan asked hopefully.

"Of course. Go visit. She's in the sitting room. I'll be right in."

Ryan stood in the doorway, a smile lighting her face. Her grandmother was facing the windows, her gaze looking out over the ocean. She'd lived here all of her life, and Ryan couldn't even begin to count the number of days her grandmother must have stared at that very sight.

"You up for company?"

Her grandmother didn't turn. "About time you got here. I thought maybe you were going to stand me up."

Ryan laughed. "I would never miss your birthday, Carmen." Her grandmother lifted a hand, beckoning her to join her. Ryan moved into the room, bending down to kiss her cheek. "You look as lovely as ever," Ryan said honestly.

Her grandmother squeezed her hand as her eyes traveled over her. She smiled, then laughed. "Oh my, but don't you look pretty."

"You like it?"

"It makes you look very handsome, if I may use that word."

"Handsome, huh?"

"Are the ladies still chasing you?"

Ryan shook her head. "Only when they know who I am."

"Still in hiding then, are you?"

"Is that what you call it?"

Her grandmother patted the seat next to her, and Ryan relaxed beside her. Her grandmother's surprisingly strong hand closed around her own.

"Are you writing, dear?"

"Actually, yes. Well, I was," she admitted.

"Summer in the mountains got you sidetracked again?"

Ryan nodded, letting her think that. "I'm not sure why I'm even bothering, though. I don't think I'll ever attempt to publish again."

"Nonsense. You have a wonderful talent, Catherine. You should not waste it."

"I believe you are the only one who thinks that. Mother still doubts me," she said.

"I'll tell you now what I told you back then. Screw her!"

Ryan laughed, waiting for the statement she always followed up with.

"I never wanted Christopher to marry her, but your grandfather thought it would be a good match." She squeezed her hand tightly. "But of course, I wouldn't have you then, would I?"

Ryan nodded. "I know I should come around more often," she said.

"Oh, now don't feel guilty. You have your own life. You and your mother are like oil and water. Always have been."

Abby interrupted them then, bringing over a tray. She poured tea into a cup and handed it to Carmen, then offered a cup of coffee to Ryan.

"You take it black, if I remember."

"Yes, thanks."

"Thank you, Abby," Carmen said. "Why don't you go relax and not worry about me. If I need something, Catherine can help me."

"Very well. Enjoy your visit."

When she was out of earshot, her grandmother leaned closer. "She hovers. I think she thinks I'm going to kick the bucket any day now."

Ryan smiled, knowing Abby was very loyal to her grandmother. "She cares about you."

"Oh, I know. But she insists I take a nap every day as if I'm old or something," she said with a quick laugh. "I don't feel eighty-nine. I guess I'm not sure what eighty-nine is supposed to feel like."

"Do you get out much, Carmen?"

"I walk the grounds every day. And Arthur is kind enough to walk with me to the gazebo. He sits with me so that I can watch the waves."

"They don't allow you to do that alone?"

"Like I said, they all think I'm at death's door. Or maybe they think I'm going to fall and break a hip or something."

"I'll take you out there if you want," Ryan offered. "I can even make myself scarce so you can have some alone time."

"I don't want alone time when you're here, Catherine. I'd much rather enjoy your company. Perhaps we could stroll down there, though. It would be nice to sit with you."

"How about we go before dinner?"

"How about we go now?" she suggested. "I assume you haven't seen her yet."

"Mother? No. Arthur said she was with the caterers. How many guests are you expecting this year?"

"Three or four hundred," she said. "Your mother is quite the event organizer. The more celebrities she has, the more cameras there are. Those entertainment shows are sending reporters again this year. My birthday has turned into a circus, hasn't it?"

"Oh, you love it or you wouldn't still do it. Besides, it brings in a lot of money, doesn't it?"

"Yes, this event raises more money for the disease than any other single event. For that I'm very proud. But I've grown weary of the annual affair. Your mother loves it, of course."

"Well, it has taken on a life of its own."

"I know. But she's going to do with it what she wants. I'm too old to protest."

Ryan heard the frustration in her grandmother's voice and knew it was time to change the subject. She stood, offering her hand. "How about that walk?"

"Yes, go grab my cane," she said. "And then you can tell me all about the mountains. I love hearing about your cabin and your dogs and your friends there."

Ryan did as instructed, already debating whether she should mention the stranded guest she harbored for nearly two months. Her grandmother would enjoy the tale, but she didn't know if she wanted to bring Jen into the conversation or not. She wasn't certain she was ready to talk about Jen to anyone.

She led Carmen slowly to the elevator that would take them down to the first floor, her thoughts still far away.

# CHAPTER TWENTY-EIGHT

Jen stood at the window, her cup of coffee long cold. She finally set it down, then brought her gaze back to the window, looking out over the rooftops of her neighbor's houses to the faint outline of the northern mountains. She couldn't focus on anything and she'd been staring out the window for most of the day.

Well, she could focus on something, but it was the one thing she *didn't* want to think about.

Ryan.

Last night had been incredible. Even the fantasies she had had couldn't compare. But for the life of her, she couldn't understand why Ryan had run. Why would she show up without warning and then just run?

Maybe that was all she wanted. Sex. Ryan had told her that before. She took what women offered her—sex—and left nothing in return. Was that all she'd done with Jen? Taken what Jen willingly gave?

No. Ryan wouldn't do that to her, she was certain. But whatever Ryan was running from she still didn't trust Jen enough to share it with her. That hurt. She trusted her enough to share her body, to make love, but that was all.

*Make love.*

Jen looked away from the window, still shocked at what had occurred. She couldn't even remember their conversation, if there'd been any. All she remembered was taking Ryan into her bedroom, offering herself to Ryan. And it was the most incredible night of her life.

It confirmed that her decision to end things with Brad had been the right one. But did it also indicate her other suspicions were correct? Was she a lesbian? Had Ryan opened up a whole new world for her? And if so, where did she go from here?

Her phone rang, bringing her out of her musings. It would be Cheryl. They'd had a lunch date planned, but Jen hadn't been in the mood to see anyone. She'd shot her a vague e-mail, canceling. No doubt Cheryl's curiosity was piqued.

Well, she couldn't talk to her yet. She let it go to voice mail. Maybe they could get together in a couple of days. Maybe she'd be ready to talk then. She smiled ruefully, picturing Cheryl's reaction to Jen's latest revelation.

# CHAPTER TWENTY-NINE

"Well, well. If it isn't Cat, returning to the nest."

Ryan turned at the sound of her brother's voice, smiling despite herself. "Chuck," she replied, using the nickname he despised.

"Catbird," he countered.

"Chucky ducky."

He laughed. "Okay, enough." He pointed at her hair. "I like it. It's good to see you."

Ryan stood, accepting the hug he offered. "Good to see you too."

"Missed you on the island this winter."

"I'm sure you did. How many women did you bring with you this time?"

"Just three." He glanced at their grandmother. "They were just friends, Carmen."

"I may be old but I'm not stupid," she said. "Why don't you join us?"

"Can't. I brought company along," he said with a wink. "But I wanted to give Cat the head's up."

She flicked her eyes to his. "About?"

"Mother has lined up an interview for you. *People* magazine."

"Mother can kiss my ass," she said vehemently.

"Just thought you should know, so she didn't just spring it on you," he said.

"Yeah. Thanks."

"Will you and your friend join us for dinner?" Carmen asked.

"Of course. I want her to meet Cat. She hasn't been here before so I wanted to show her around."

They waved him off, but Ryan was stewing over his words. Her mother was still clueless about how much that whole episode hurt her. Now, on the ten-year anniversary of her Pulitzer, she wanted to schedule an interview? Never.

"I didn't know about the interview or I would have told you myself," Carmen said.

"Why would she do that to me? It's ancient history; I've tried to put it behind me. Why does she want to bring it up?"

"Oh, sweet Catherine, you know how your mother is. Any publicity will do."

Ryan nodded. "That's why I live where I do. I'm not a *name* there. I just want to be left in peace."

Her grandmother surprised her with her question. "Do you get lonely, Catherine?"

She turned away, her gaze drifting to the surf. "I used to not, no," she said honestly. "This summer though, it's been tough," she admitted.

"You've met someone, haven't you?"

Ryan looked at her grandmother quickly, astonished that she would draw that conclusion.

"You have a different look about you this time," Carmen explained. "Normally, you just look bored when you're here; you go through the motions. Today, though, you have an almost wistful look on your face." She took her hand again. "Want to share with your old grandmother?"

Ryan smiled. "Her name is Jen. She stayed with me for two months as winter turned to spring."

"Ah. I see."

"No. It wasn't like that. She was stranded. Got her car caught in an avalanche," she explained. "I guess I got used to her company."

"And are you and this Jen lovers?"

Ryan felt her stomach flip over, picturing Jen as just that. Her lover. But she shook her head. "She left when the snow melted."

"As I told Charles, I may be old but I'm not stupid."

Ryan stood, pacing. "No, but I think I may be."

"Want to tell me?"

"She lives in Santa Fe. I stopped off there on my way here," she said. Her grandmother's eyes watched her, but she said nothing. "She's got a life. She's got a boyfriend who wants to marry her. Whatever attraction there was between us, it's all new to her. She doesn't need this in her life."

"So you stopped off there...why, then?"

Ryan looked back to the waves, staring at them. "I just had to see her." She shoved her hands in her pockets and took a few steps away. "We slept together."

"You slept together? With this woman who has a boyfriend?"

Ryan nodded.

"And is she one of these women who do that sort of thing because of your name?"

Ryan raised an eyebrow and Carmen laughed. "Of course I know what goes on, dear. The Ryan-Barrett name is very powerful."

But Ryan shook her head. "Jen doesn't know who I am."

"Then why?"

That simple question made Ryan consider it fully. Yes, why had Jen slept with her? Why had Jen allowed all that had happened between them? Why was her touch so tender and affectionate? She turned away from what she feared was the truth.

"I don't know why," she said instead. "I just don't know."

***

"Oh...my God. What have you done to yourself?"

"Hello, Mother."

"Your...your hair. It looks positively hideous, you must know that."

"Yes, I'm doing well. It's so good to see you too," Ryan said sarcastically as she led Carmen to the dinner table.

"Surely you don't plan to go out in public looking like that? Do you have any idea how many guests we'll be having tomorrow? And media," she added, as if that mattered.

"Since I've already paid my respects to Carmen, I don't imagine it's imperative that I be there anyway," she said with a shrug. "I can just head back home."

"Of course it's imperative. Did you do this just to embarrass me?"

Ryan laughed. "Charles whores around town, yet my haircut embarrasses you? I think that's a bit skewed, don't you?"

Her mother turned to Arthur, who had been standing patiently behind her. "Call in Tommy. Tell him we have an emergency. Maybe he can fix her up."

"Who's Tommy?" Ryan asked.

"He's my hairdresser. Perhaps he can find a wig or something for this."

"Mother, your hairdresser is not touching me. And if you think I'm wearing a wig, you're out of your fucking mind." She pulled out a chair for Carmen, surprised by the smile playing on her grandmother's face.

"Do not speak like that in this house, Catherine. I don't know what kind of company you keep out there," she said with a wave of her hand, "but we don't use that word in this house."

"What's all the yelling about this time?" Charles said as he and his current flame walked in. "I'll guess the hair," he said.

"Can you believe she did that to herself?"

"I like it," he said. "Cat, this is Presley Stewart. Presley, my sister Catherine."

"It's so nice to finally meet you," Presley said as she shook Ryan's hand.

"Thanks. You too," Ryan said politely.

"And this is my grandmother, Carmen. And this lovely lady is my mother, Vanessa."

"Nice to meet you both," Presley said with a bit of a nervous smile on her face.

"Lovely to have you here, dear. Please sit," Vanessa instructed.

Charles pulled out a chair for Presley, looking around the table as he did so. "We seem to be missing someone," he said.

"Your father had...urgent business to attend to."

Ryan and Charles exchanged glances, both knowing that was their mother's way of telling them he was with his mistress. Ryan wondered why he couldn't have made an exception, seeing as how she only visited once a year. But then again, could she blame him? His alternative was spending time with her mother. She reached for her wineglass, wishing Sophie would hurry with the meal.

"I assume you have everything in order for tomorrow," Carmen said.

"Of course. It's been in order for weeks now. Do you think I would allow something to slip through the cracks?"

Ryan felt the tension in the room and glanced over at Presley, offering an apologetic smile. She was shocked at the flirtatious look she received in return.

"Can we please skip all the drama?" Charles asked. "We have company after all," he said, motioning to Presley.

"Of course, darling. Forgive me, Presley. This is just a stressful time for me—trying to put together Carmen's birthday party. Something always goes wrong." She looked over at Ryan. "Like my daughter thinking she looks good in a man's haircut."

There were so many things Ryan wanted to say, but she clamped her mouth shut. She reminded herself it was like this every year. Her mother always found something wrong with her. She always had. By the time Ryan reached fifteen, she'd stopped trying to please her.

"I like her hair," Carmen said. "She looks...smart."

"I like it too," Presley said shyly. "It's very attractive on you."

Ryan kept her expression even as she looked from Presley to Charles, waiting for her mother's response.

"Attractive? I know my daughter thinks she's gay, but must she advertise it so?"

Ryan bit her lip, vowing—again—that this would be the last year she came here.

Charles gasped in mock surprise. "Gay? *Catbird?* You must be joking, Mother."

Vanessa looked smugly over at Ryan. "It's a shame you're not more outgoing like your brother. He, at least, has a social life."

Ryan turned to her grandmother. "Why do I put myself through this every year?" she murmured.

Her grandmother smiled sweetly at her, and Ryan of course knew the answer.

"By the way, I'll need you to be available at ten tomorrow morning," her mother said.

Ryan looked up. "Who? Me?"

"Yes, you."

Ryan shook her head. "No. Whatever it is, no."

"Catherine, you have obligations to this family, you know that."

Ryan looked at her skeptically. "And what family obligation will I be filling?"

"There is a gentleman who wishes to speak with you. It should only take a half hour at most."

"And would this gentleman happen to be a reporter?"

Vanessa glared at Charles, who had the good sense not to crack a joke at that particular moment.

"Like I said, it shouldn't take more than a half hour."

"And like I said, no."

To her relief, Arthur escorted Sophie in with the serving cart at that point, and conversation halted as she served everyone. The lamb chop looked delicious, but Ryan's appetite had vanished long ago.

"Thank you, Sophie. The plate looks lovely," Vanessa said, dismissing her. Arthur followed obediently behind.

"This is perfect, as always," Charles said as he took a bite. "She's an excellent cook."

Ryan agreed but knew she wouldn't do the meal justice. Oh, how she wished she were back in the mountains, finishing up an evening hike with the dogs. She imagined walking inside her cabin to the smell of dinner on the stove...and Jen waiting for her.

"Why are you opposed to an interview?" her mother asked, pulling her back to the present.

"Mother, surely you know the answer to that."

"Well, if you insist you wrote the book, why won't you give an interview to tell your side of things?"

"Why should I have to tell my side? I wrote the book under a pseudonym to avoid publicity and to avoid the scrutiny that my name would cause. Lot of good that did."

"Did you ever find out who leaked your name?" Charles asked.

"I can only guess. There were four people with that knowledge. The only one I trusted was my editor."

"If I may ask, what are you talking about? What book?" Presley asked.

Charles glanced at Ryan, but Ryan shook her head. She was in no mood to get into all that now.

"I'll explain later," Charles said. "So Carmen, I heard that after you turn ninety, you're going to cease having these birthday parties. Is that true?"

"Stop them? Of course we're not stopping them," Vanessa said dismissively. "This is an opportunity to show—" She stopped, apparently remembering they had a guest. "Regardless, we're not stopping them."

"Wow, Carmen, it's like you're a ventriloquist. I never once saw your mouth move," Charles said with a laugh.

Ryan smiled too, knowing her brother was the only one who could get away with talking to their mother that way. She finished her glass of wine, hoping Arthur would come around soon to offer refills. As if reading her mind, he magically appeared, wine bottle in hand. She nodded at his silent request, waiting while he poured.

"I'll have a bit more too, Arthur. Thank you," Carmen said.

"Carmen? Do you think that's wise?" Vanessa asked.

"I enjoy my wine, Vanessa. You know that," she said. "Besides, I don't believe there's a maximum age limit." She took a sip and gingerly put the glass back down. "By the way, I *do* intend on stopping my birthday parties after next year. If you wish to continue the fundraiser, that's your business, of course," she said. "But you'll have to pick a different time of year for it and a different name."

"Christopher has said no such thing to me," Vanessa said.

"I don't believe that Christopher's name is on the banner outside, now is it?"

Ryan wanted to applaud her grandmother but seeing her mother's look of disbelief was enough.

"Are they exhausting for you?" Ryan asked.

"Yes. And they keep getting bigger and lasting longer," she said with a glance at Vanessa.

*As is this dinner*, Ryan thought as she sipped her wine. She looked across the table, finding Presley's gaze on her. She smiled politely at the other woman, wondering at her obvious interest. While it had happened before, it wasn't often that one of Charles' dates strayed from him to her.

Conversation was sparse; her mother appeared to be sulking. After what seemed an eternity, dessert was served, which Ryan declined. She was surprised her brother did as well.

"Join me in the study, Cat. We'll catch up."

She arched an eyebrow, thinking it terribly rude of him to ditch his date, but she agreed with a nod. Her father's study was quite large, housing not only his desk and credenza but a conference table as well. Charles went to the liquor cabinet, holding up a bottle for her inspection.

"Cognac. Nice," she said with a nod.

"You still like living in the mountains?"

"Love it," she said, taking the glass he offered.

"Do you miss Aspen?"

She laughed. "Don't miss the crowds, no. You still go skiing there?"

"Yes. I went this winter. Missed seeing you there," he said.

"I was looking for something with a little more solitude and a lot less trendiness."

He sat down in her father's chair, and she pulled out one of the guest chairs. "My date seems to have her eye on you," he said.

She nodded. "Noticed that, did you?"

"I'm shocked. She's a little hellcat in bed, if you know what I mean."

"She looks to be ten years younger than you."

He grinned. "Eleven."

"Where'd you meet her?"

"At a party, where else?" He eyed her. "You interested?"

"In her?"

He raised his eyebrows. "I could watch."

"You're insane."

"We did it before. Remember that chick I brought home from college? What were you? Eighteen?"

"The difference is, I didn't *know* you were watching," she reminded him. She'd never been more embarrassed in her young life when she found out he'd been hiding in the closet. She'd already learned by then that her name could get her anything—anyone—she wanted. She just had no idea that included her brother's girlfriends. Thankfully, Charles didn't care. He'd already been entrenched in his playboy ways and *always* had a backup. She was, however, careful to check her closet from then on.

"Well, you can have her if you want her," he said, giving her permission. "I'm not really that into her. All she wanted was a ticket to the party tomorrow." He downed the last of his drink before reaching for the bottle again. "I'd rather cruise the party anyway," he said.

"I'm not interested," she said.

"No? She's got a body to die for. Did I mention her stamina?" He laughed. "God, it's like she could go all night."

"You're a pig," she said with a grin.

Arthur tapped on the door before opening it. "Charles, dessert is finished. I thought I'd bring Miss Presley around to you."

"Of course, Arthur. Thank you."

"I hope I'm not interrupting," she said.

"No, of course not. Would you like a glass?" Ryan offered.

"Oh, I'd love one," she purred.

Ryan looked up, her eyes meeting Presley's, acknowledging the invitation she found there. To her surprise, she wasn't at all interested. She finished her drink and put the glass on the desk.

"I'll let you two get to it then. I'm very tired. I'll see you in the morning." She didn't miss the disappointed expression on Presley's face, but the truth was, she wasn't tempted in the least. She was, however, a bit surprised at her reasoning. She didn't want anything to erase the still fresh memories of Jen. She didn't want another woman touching her, kissing her. And she didn't want her hands on another woman.

She wanted Jen.

# CHAPTER THIRTY

"Yes, we'll do an early dinner," Jen said, making up for her missed lunch with Cheryl. "I'll be there by six."

She'd avoided Cheryl for two days. She'd avoided Brad as well. In fact, she hadn't left the house. To be honest, she hadn't done much of anything. Except replay her time with Ryan. Like an old movie reel, over and over it played. Her body still tingled when she thought of Ryan's hands on her, touching her, bringing her alive, all of her senses buzzing, all of her wants and desires being satisfied by Ryan's hands...and mouth.

The flame still burned. Ryan hadn't totally doused it. She kept hoping Ryan would come back, would show up again unannounced, standing on her doorstep waiting for Jen to let her inside again.

She knew that wasn't going to happen. Ryan had run from her. Why she ran, Jen still had no idea. She had most likely fled back home to the mountains where she felt safe. Jen had picked up the phone countless times, wanting to call Morgan, wanting to talk. But she reminded herself that Morgan was Ryan's friend, not hers. Morgan's loyalty was to Ryan. So she'd dealt with it alone, going from disbelief to acceptance in two days. Disbelief that she'd slept with another woman, and accepting that she wanted to do it again.

But not with just any woman.

With Ryan.

# CHAPTER THIRTY-ONE

The crowd was electric and lively, and Ryan moved through it, nodding at familiar faces, not pausing to visit. The speeches were over, and now the alcohol flowed with tuxedoed waiters making the rounds with silver trays. She deposited her champagne glass and made her way to the bar. She spied Charles doing the same with Presley right on his heels.

"Carmen gave another great speech, didn't she?"

Ryan nodded, offering a quick smile to Presley. "She's a pro. Mother, on the other hand, was as obnoxious as ever."

"Scotch?"

"Sure."

Presley still sipped from her champagne glass. She eased closer to Ryan as Charles went to the bar. "How long are you staying?"

"At the party?"

"No, here. Will you be here a few more days? I have some time. I'd love to get to know you better."

Ryan was shocked at how forward she was, especially with Charles nearby. She looked her over, noting again how beautiful she was: flawless skin, makeup applied to perfection, blond and thin, young and energetic. If this had been last year, Ryan would have already had her in bed. But this wasn't last year.

"I appreciate the offer," she said, "but you should stick with Charles. Besides, I'm leaving in the morning. Early."

"Pity. We could have had fun."

"Fun? I guess I'm getting old then." She leaned closer. "A quick fuck, just to get off, isn't really fun to me anymore. If that's all I need, I can take care of that myself."

Presley smiled seductively. "That's a nice visual. But surely it's more fun if you have help with that?"

Ryan laughed. "You don't give up, do you?"

"You intrigue me."

"Why? You're straight."

She shrugged. "Yes. But I've had many lovers, both men and women."

Ryan looked up as a TV camera scanned the crowd; she turned away from it, taking Presley with her. Charles returned, handing Ryan her drink.

"I see you're as shy as ever. Why do you think they try so hard to get a shot of you?" he asked. "Me? I don't run from them, so they don't even bother anymore."

"Well, I don't want to be on the cover of some tabloid next week and have quotes made about me *by a friend of the family*," she said. "Besides, you love being on tabloid covers."

"Yeah, but I haven't had any drunken encounters with tabloid reporters lately. Old news anyway." He glanced at Presley. "I have a reputation to uphold, you know."

She nodded and smiled. "I love bad boys." She looked at Ryan. "And girls."

Charles laughed. "Very subtle, Presley."

"She's already turned me down."

Charles looked at Ryan questioningly, but Ryan shook her head. "As much as I'm enjoying the conversation, I think I'll go spend some time with Carmen," Ryan said.

"That means she's had enough of the party and is going to sneak up to her room," Charles said.

Ryan nodded. "Alone. See you at breakfast."

She made her way through the throng of guests, spotting her grandmother chatting with Senator Reynolds. Instead of interrupting, she turned, threading her way across the manicured lawn and back up to the mansion.

Once in her room, she kicked off her shoes and slipped out of the designer suit, tossing it across the settee. She hated these events with a passion. She hated playing dress-up, she hated schmoozing with the rich and famous, she hated the politics involved in it all.

She took a quick shower, wanting nothing more than for the night to be over so that she could head back home. She missed Sierra and Kia. She missed Reese and Morgan. She missed the quiet of the mountains. She missed her daily hikes. She missed the sunset from the ridge.

And God, she missed Jen.

# CHAPTER THIRTY-TWO

"You brought wine?" Cheryl asked with a grin. "What's gotten into you?"

"I know it's a bottle you enjoy," Jen said. "And I may need it," she added.

"Oh? What's up?"

Jen shrugged. "Just need to talk."

Cheryl nodded. "That's what friends are for. Why don't we go ahead and open it?" she said as she took out two wineglasses. "Turn the TV off for me, would you? I was watching the news earlier."

Jen walked around the bar, finding the remote next to Cheryl's recliner. Just as she was about to click it off, her eyes were drawn to the TV. She nearly dropped the remote as she fumbled with the sound.

*"Catherine Ryan-Barrett made a rare public appearance, caught here chatting with her brother, Charles. Unlike the rest of the family, Catherine shuns the limelight, usually only appearing at her grandmother's annual charity event. Her mother, Vanessa, was seen..."*

"Dear God," she murmured. "I can't believe it."

"What is it?" Cheryl asked, glancing at the TV. "Oh. The rich pretending to be concerned with a cause. I can't stand her."

"Who?"

"Vanessa Ryan-Barrett. The mother. She's so full of herself. Thinks she's a celebrity or something."

Jen clicked the TV off, turning to Cheryl. "It's...it's her."

"Who?"

"Ryan. It's...Ryan."

"What are you talking about? *Your* Ryan?"

"Yes. Catherine," she said, the name sounding strange to her.

"The daughter? Catherine? She's the one who rescued you?"

"Yes." Jen looked around. "Where's your laptop?"

"Over there. Why?"

"Because I don't even know who she is," she said quickly.

"The Ryan-Barrett family owns the R&B hotel chain. They also own a casino, I think." Cheryl stared at her. "You're a writer. How can you not know about Catherine Ryan-Barrett?"

"I just don't," she said as she pulled up Google. She scanned the page, trying to decide on which link to click on when she saw the word *Pulitzer*. "Seriously? A Pulitzer?" She clicked on it, then glanced at Cheryl. "What do you know about her?"

Cheryl brought over a wineglass for her, then sat down beside her. "Oh, there was some scandal about her Pulitzer. It's been a number of years ago now."

"Ten," Jen said as she read the article. "*Dancing on the Moon*. She wrote it under a pseudonym. M.P. Turner."

"That's right. After it won a Pulitzer, her publisher leaked her real name."

"And the book lost credibility immediately," Jen said, quoting what she read. "Ryan-Barrett denied allegations that a ghostwriter penned the book, as did her publisher."

"They made a fortune on the book what with all the publicity," Cheryl said. "I would have never read it otherwise. I'm glad I did. It was very well written."

Jen slammed the laptop closed and stared at Cheryl. "She's a *writer*."

Cheryl looked at her quizzically. "Yes. That's what we've been talking about."

"No. I mean, she's a writer. A *real* writer." She stood, angry now. "And she didn't tell me. I'm going on and on about my silly little self-help books and she's a *writer*," she finished loudly.

"They're not silly," Cheryl insisted. "And I'm not saying that just because I work for your publisher," she said with a grin.

"She probably thought I was an idiot." She shook her head. "She won a Pulitzer, for God's sake. Why wouldn't she tell me?"

"I don't know. You said the woman you met was a recluse. From all accounts, Catherine is very reclusive. And she didn't tell you her real name. I'm assuming she didn't want you to know about that part of her life."

Jen just stared at her, finally blurting out, "I slept with her."

Cheryl nearly spit out her wine. "*What*? When?"

Jen sat down again, her hands shaking as she took a large sip of wine. "Wednesday night. She showed up at my house."

"And you...you slept with her? Like had sex?"

"Yes like had sex," Jen snapped. "I'm such a fool."

"You're not a fool. You didn't know who she was."

"Why would she do that? Why would she come to my house and...God, it was so special, Cheryl. At least for me. Apparently not for her." Jen turned away. "She left before I woke up. Left me a note. She just said she was sorry, and she hoped I didn't hate her."

"Did she mean like now, when you found out who she was?"

"I don't think so. I think she meant for," Jen smiled, "taking my virtue. That and for leaving. I don't think she anticipated me finding out who she was." Jen blew out her breath. "I don't care who she is. I don't even *know* who she is."

"Are you in love with her?" Cheryl asked gently.

"I feel *something*, yes," Jen admitted. And making love with Ryan, the way Ryan looked at her, she would have sworn Ryan felt something too. Maybe that was why she ran.

"What are you going to do?"

Yes, what was she going to do? Call Morgan? Drive back up to the mountains? But what if Ryan didn't want to see her? What if all she wanted...was what Jen had already given her?

She shrugged. "I don't know what I'm going to do."

# CHAPTER THIRTY-THREE

"You *slept* with her? And then you just *left?*"

Ryan nodded, almost afraid to look at Morgan. "I didn't know what to do."

Morgan shook her head. "How about sticking around long enough to talk about it. God, you simply amaze me." She squatted down beside her. "Ryan, you know I love you. And I say this with the utmost affection. But you, my friend, are an idiot." She stood. "An idiot."

"What did I do? I went there, hoping that we could talk, catch up. The next thing I know, we're naked and—"

"And you left. What about Jen? How do you think she felt the next morning when she woke up and you were gone? How do you think she felt when she read the lame-ass note you left? You know she's never been with a woman before. You know how new this is for her." Morgan shook her head again. "She probably doesn't have anyone to talk to. She probably needed to talk about what happened. But you left."

"I didn't know what else to do."

"Come on, Ryan. You had sex with her. She's not some bimbo you met on the ski slopes. This is Jen. Why would you leave?"

"Hell, I don't know. She may be engaged by now. I didn't need to stick around. I know I probably already screwed up her life. I didn't need to hang around and talk about it."

"I swear, you are clueless. She's not engaged."

"How do you know?"

"Because she told me how she felt about him...what's his name? Brad? She told me she wasn't in love with him. She wasn't going to marry the guy. You. You were the one she was attracted to. You. You big idiot."

Ryan watched Morgan huff off, and she turned to Reese who hadn't said a word. "Anything to add?"

Reese smiled. "No. I think Morgan pretty much covered it."

"So you think I'm an idiot too?"

"All I know is, when I picked her up that day, the last thing that woman wanted was to be leaving with me."

Ryan looked into the eyes of her friend. "I'm scared."

Reese nodded. "Are you in love with her?"

Ryan looked away. Was she? She shrugged. "I don't guess I've ever been in love before. Because I've never felt like this before." She looked away, staring out into the forest behind their deck. "It was incredible. She was so...so innocent and trusting. My God, we spent hours together. It was incredible." She took a deep breath. "And I panicked. I totally panicked. I thought, what have I done? Jen doesn't need this in her life. Doesn't need me. So I ran. I told myself it would be better for her, you know. It's better if I left. She could go back to her life, I could go back to mine. You know, she's got a life there. She's got friends there. She's got...*Brad*," she said. "What do I have to offer? I'm up here. This feels like home to me. I feel alive up here."

"She makes you feel alive, doesn't she?"

Ryan slowly nodded. "Like never before."

*** 

"You could hang around here a few days," Morgan offered the next morning. "Cody has certainly enjoyed having the girls here."

Ryan followed her gaze to where the three dogs were playfully fighting over one of Cody's toys. She was tempted to stay. The thought of going up to the cabin—alone—was unsettling. But she couldn't put it off forever.

"Maybe I'll stay one more night," she conceded. "But I'll pick up some steaks at Lou's. You know how Reese likes to sit out and grill."

"Deal."

Ryan sipped her coffee, wondering why Morgan hadn't left for work yet. "You staying home today?"

Morgan nodded. "It's Monday. Not a lot going on. Tina and Greg can handle things."

"Babysitting me?" she guessed.

Morgan smiled. "I thought you might want to talk."

"Are you going to yell at me again?"

"No." Morgan sat across from her, sipping her own coffee. "Did she like your hair?"

Ryan remembered Jen's fingers as they brushed through it. "Yes. Yes she did." She cleared her throat, then looked at Morgan. "I'm not...I'm not strong enough, Morgan."

Morgan's eyes softened as she nodded. "Yes, you are."

"No. I couldn't chance it. I couldn't possibly go see her again. I couldn't take the rejection."

Morgan reached across the table, taking her hand. "Ryan, why do you think Jen would reject you? Jen...she's not like the others. She doesn't know who you are. She doesn't care what your name is."

"No. I couldn't take the chance. It would break my heart."

Morgan pulled her hand away. "Yeah. Well, just think about *yourself*, why don't you? What about Jen? Do you think about her? You've probably already broken her heart."

Ryan shook her head. "You don't know that."

"She's in love with you. She was already in love with you when she left here. Why do you think she was crying?"

Ryan stared at her, speechless.

"Don't let this chance pass you by, Ryan. Love doesn't come around often. You've got to grab it when it does." She shook her head slowly. "You know how Reese and I met. You know our story. We were both too stubborn to admit we'd fallen in love and had broken our silly no-strings agreement."

"This is different."

"Is it? Love is love, Ryan."

Ryan stood up, walking away from the table. "Is it love, Morgan? Is it really? We spent two months together and shared one kiss. We slept together. Is it love?"

"You really are terrified, aren't you?"

"I feel like my life is coming unraveled," she admitted. "My safe, solitary life...the life I've grown to love, is coming apart at the seams. So, yes, I'm terrified." She shoved the chair against the table. "I've got to get it back. We'll take a rain check on steaks, okay? I need to...I just need to go. Get back to the cabin."

Ryan whistled for the dogs, then did what she did best. She ran away.

# CHAPTER THIRTY-FOUR

Jen stared at the picture, memorizing every detail. She didn't know why she was torturing herself, but she couldn't help it. The camera had caught Ryan unaware, her attention on the young woman beside her. Jen refused to speculate on who the blonde was, keeping her attention on Ryan instead. *Catherine.* She shook her head. No, it was Ryan. She would always be Ryan to her.

Her phone rang and she glanced at the number, not recognizing it. She closed her laptop before answering.

"Jen Kincaid," she said.

"Jen, hi. This is Morgan, from Colorado. You may not remember me, I'm—"

"Of course I remember you." She paused, feeling her pulse race to life nervously. "How is she?"

"Not great," Morgan said.

"That makes two of us."

"I figured as much."

"I suppose she told you?"

"Yes. She didn't mean to hurt you, Jen. She thought she was doing the right thing."

"By leaving me? By coming here and...and...and then just leaving?"

"I know. You've got to understand. She's—"

"She's running," Jen said. "She's been running. That's why she lives the way she does." Jen took a deep breath. "I know who she is. I saw...I saw her on TV. I saw her face and I couldn't believe it was her. Now I know what she's been running from. And I understand why she didn't tell me who she was. I know she didn't want me to judge her. But to me, she's still just *Ryan*."

"She told me she was afraid to tell you. She said she was afraid you'd think she was a fraud."

"I would never think that. I don't care who she is. I don't care about all that." She stared off into space. "I feel so empty inside, Morgan. I miss her so much." She bit her lip, knowing what she needed to do. "I want to see her." She took a deep breath, hesitating. "Do you think that's a good idea? Do you think I should come up? I mean, I couldn't bear the rejection if she just sent me away. I think I'd rather live with the *what if's* than to go up there and have her send me away."

"She won't send you away, Jen. She's fallen hard for you, it seems."

Jen closed her eyes, not daring to believe it. "I'm afraid."

"Yes, so is she. Jen, Ryan's not one for talking. She's used to running. Right now, I think she's terrified of how she feels. I know she regrets what she did, but she still thinks what she did was best for you. I talked to her some, but she left here the other day in a panic. We haven't heard from her since."

"She's hiding," Jen said, knowing with certainty that Ryan was.

"Yes. Unfortunately she can't hide from herself."

# CHAPTER THIRTY-FIVE

Ryan stood at the window, watching the day dawn over her little slice of heaven. Only it hadn't exactly felt like heaven to her in months. She glanced down, seeing both dogs watching her.

"I miss her," she said.

Sierra tilted her head, listening.

"You probably miss her too." She was almost disappointed when she got no response.

She went to the kitchen, tossing out her cold coffee and refilling her cup—her third of the morning already. The silence in the cabin was deafening. Each day, it seemed to get louder and louder. So much so that she spent nearly every daylight hour outside, hiking, moving around, anything to keep from being alone in the cabin.

She rarely opened her laptop, rarely turned on the TV. She was in a funk and she knew it. She should go down the mountain, hang out with Morgan and Reese for a few days, hang out at Sloan's Bar. Hell, drive to Gunnison or something. Anything to escape the silent hell she found herself in.

But she hadn't spoken with Morgan or Reese since the day she fled. Morgan's words still rang in her ears.

*"She's in love with you. She was already in love with you when she left here. Why do you think she was crying?"*

Had Jen fallen in love with her? Was that possible? Did she dare believe that someone could love her? Love *her*, not love her name. If she was being completely honest with herself, she would admit that yes, Jen had taken her heart when she left here. And had locked it up even tighter after she'd visited her in Santa Fe.

Visited? No, they hadn't visited. They'd made love. Over and over. They hadn't talked. Not really.

*We made love.*

Ryan closed her eyes, remembering Jen's touch, remembering it like it was yesterday. Yet it seemed so long ago since she'd seen her, touched her, felt her.

She ached for her still. Ached to hear her voice. Ached to touch her. Ached to have Jen touch her. Ached to make love with her again.

She put her cup down, walking purposefully to the door. She did what she did best.

She ran.

Ran from her thoughts. Ran from herself.

"Come on, girls."

They burst out the door with her, out into the fresh air, away from the stifling silence of the cabin. She shut her thoughts off and headed down the mountain, hoping to find some peace.

# CHAPTER THIRTY-SIX

Nothing looked familiar. It had been four months since she left, and the bright colors of summer had replaced the snow she remembered piled high on the side of the road. Thanks to Reese's precise directions, though, she had no chance to take a wrong turn.

Jen gripped the steering wheel tightly, still not knowing what she was going to say to Ryan. She had tried to imagine Ryan's reaction to her visit, and she just couldn't. Part of her was afraid Ryan would tell her to leave. After all, this was her sanctuary. She lived a solitary life by choice. Jen didn't want to assume Ryan would let her in. She hadn't had a choice during the winter when Jen was stuck here. Now? She might tell Jen to head right back to Santa Fe. And that, of course, would break her.

Cheryl told her she was crazy to come up here, saying Jen was only asking for heartache. Maybe she was. But she couldn't leave things as they were. She couldn't let Ryan just run from her. Although she did try to prepare herself for the possibility that Ryan wouldn't want her here, that Ryan would ask her to leave.

She was well past where her rented SUV had been buried by the avalanche. She glanced again at Reese's map, slowing when she saw a road to the right. She turned off the forest road, seeing the posted Private Property signs, knowing she would soon come upon the cabin.

Her heart beat nervously. She swallowed her apprehension, knowing she was doing the right thing. Knowing that didn't help ease her nerves, though. She bounced along the dirt road, making note of the landmarks Reese had told her to look for. It all looked so different when it was not buried in snow.

Finally, she saw it. The cabin. A black Jeep was parked to the side under one of the pines. She stopped her rental next to it, sitting still for several minutes, thinking Ryan would come out if she heard her. There was no movement, however, so she got out, her legs shaking with nervousness.

"You're being ridiculous," she muttered, although that did little to temper her uneasiness.

She paused at the door, knocking politely and waiting. Still nothing. She had a moment of panic, knowing Morgan and Reese hadn't talked to Ryan in over a week. What if something had happened to her? What if she was injured? What if—

She shook her thoughts away, making her way around the cabin to the deck. She peered in through the windows, finding the inside as empty as she expected. Nothing looked disturbed or out of place.

She turned around on the deck, taking in the view, a view that always put her at ease for some reason. The sun was sinking lower, signaling the end to the day. Jen nodded, knowing immediately where she'd find Ryan.

She hurried around the cabin, finding the trail that would take her to the ridge...and the sunset. The altitude was affecting her; she had to stop several times to catch her breath. Finally, she crested the ridge, the sight before her making her stop in her tracks.

Ryan stood at the edge, facing west, her body silhouetted by the setting sun. Sierra and Kia stood beside her, one on either side, appearing to be watching the sunset, as enthralled by the sight as their master was. Jen stood spellbound as she watched them. She didn't move, letting Ryan finish the show alone. How many times had Jen caught a sunset, always imagining Ryan just like this, standing on the ridge as she watched the day draw to a close.

*I'm in love with her.*

Just before the sun slipped totally behind the mountain, Sierra turned, spotting her. Jen held her breath as first Sierra, then Kia ran toward her, both barking a warning until they drew nearer, near enough to recognize her. Then tails wagged and both dogs jostled for attention around her legs.

She laughed, not realizing how much she'd missed them too. She finally looked up, feeling Ryan approaching as well. They stood there for countless seconds, neither speaking.

Jen stepped forward, saying the first thing that came to mind.

"I refuse to call you Catherine."

Ryan stared at her. "You know?"

"Knowing what your name is doesn't change anything, Ryan. At least not for me." She tilted her head. "Why did you run?"

"I panicked. I just...I panicked. I thought I'd ruined your life."

Jen nodded. "You did. You did ruin my life, Ryan. I'd just spent the most incredible, wonderful, beautiful night of my life, only to find you gone the next morning. You ran. I needed you there so badly the next morning. But you left me."

"I'm so sorry, Jen. I didn't know...if Brad was still in the picture. I thought maybe you were engaged. I just don't know. I panicked."

"Do you think I could have made love to you like that if I was planning to marry someone?"

Ryan shrugged. "I just didn't know, Jen. I'm not used to this. I'm sorry." She shoved her hands in her pockets. Jen wondered if it was to stop herself from coming closer, to perhaps touch her. Ryan looked around. "How did you find me?"

Jen smiled. "The sunset. Where else would you be?"

Ryan smiled too. "You think you know me, huh?"

Jen nodded. "I think I know you, the *real* you, better than anyone else does." She took another step closer, amused by the frightened look in Ryan's eyes. "Isn't this where we're supposed to hug or something?"

"I'm scared, Jen. I'm scared of this."

"Me too."

"I missed you...so much. It's like I can't get you out of my mind."

"Then stop trying so hard to."

Ryan looked away again. "Did you think of me?"

Jen nodded. "Daily. Nightly."

Ryan looked back at her. "What happened with Brad?"

"I told him I wasn't in love with him."

Ryan nodded. "You broke his heart?"

"No. He knew. We've remained friends." She kicked absently at a rock, wondering how much she could push Ryan without having her run. "So, are we just going to stand out here and visit? Or do you want me to leave? Or what? I don't want to assume anything with you, Ryan." Their eyes met, and Jen wouldn't let her look away. "Please tell me what you're thinking."

Ryan still held her gaze. "I want to hold you and kiss you and never let you go."

"Then I suggest you do that."

****

Ryan looked down at Jen, seeing the anticipation in her eyes. She was so lovely, still looked so innocent, so trusting. There were so many things they needed to talk about but right now, with Jen lying naked in her bed, she didn't want to talk about anything.

"What are you thinking?"

"I was thinking how beautiful you look," she said.

Jen held her hand out, waiting until Ryan took it. "Don't be afraid," Jen said.

"I'm afraid you're going to break my heart," she admitted.

Jen shook her head. "No. I promise. Remember when I told you what I had with Brad wasn't enough? That there had to be more?"

Ryan nodded.

"*This*...is the more I was looking for. You." She smiled and tugged on Ryan's hand. "Now, come to bed."

Ryan pushed her fears aside, wanting nothing more than to give herself to Jen. She'd been so terribly lonely since Jen had left. She'd had four months to sort out her feelings, four months to admit—and accept—that Jen had stolen her heart without even knowing it. And now here Jen was, offering herself. Offering her love.

As Ryan settled on top of her, her thoughts weren't on the present, but on the first time they'd made love. Jen, so tentative, yet so strong, was so sure of what she wanted. Ryan had been the one unsure. Not much had changed there, she noted, as Jen pulled her closer, her legs parting, making room for Ryan.

"I was afraid I would never get to touch you again," she admitted as her lips moved to Jen's mouth.

Jen moaned into the kiss, her mouth opening, letting Ryan inside. Jen's hands weren't still as they moved across her back, then lower, cupping Ryan and pulling her even closer to her body. Ryan raised herself, trailing kisses across Jen's neck, her throat, moving to her breast.

"I love how you kiss me," Jen murmured, holding Ryan at her breast.

Ryan teased her nipple with her tongue, feeling it harden even more before closing over it, gently suckling as Jen pushed up against her, her hips moving slowly against her own.

Ryan pulled her mouth away, looking into Jen's hooded eyes, seeing desire—seeing love. She kissed the lips that were parted as her thigh nudged Jen's legs farther apart. She could feel Jen's wetness on her skin as she pressed into her. Jen moaned again, capturing Ryan's hips and pulling her hard against her.

Ryan reached between them, opening Jen to her. Their clits met and Jen's head fell back, her eyes closing as she rocked against Ryan.

"Feels so good," Jen whispered. "So good."

Ryan balanced her weight on her arms, stroking Jen's clit with her own, their wetness blending together. Ryan's breathing was as ragged as Jen's, her heart pounding fast in her chest as she moved against her, slower at first, then faster—harder—both of them moaning with each thrust. Far too soon, her orgasm threatened, and she knew she was about to climax. Her body was damp with perspiration as she continued to push into Jen, watching with satisfaction as Jen struggled to draw breath, the pleasure evident on her face. Their eyes met and held as they moved together in unison.

Two, three more strokes and Jen finally screamed out, her hands gripping tightly to Ryan's hips. Ryan let herself go, pressing hard into Jen as her own orgasm washed over her, wave after wave of pleasure soaking into her soul.

Her arms gave way and she collapsed on top of Jen, their breath mingling as they held each other.

"I love you," Ryan murmured against her mouth.

Jen held her tighter as her breathing slowed. "I love you."

# CHAPTER THIRTY-SEVEN

"So an editor?" Jen laughed. "That's the best you could come up with?"

Ryan tipped her beer bottle in her direction. "As soon as I said it, I was like, what the *hell* are you thinking?"

Her smile tempered a bit. "I wish you would have told me. Then I really could have picked your brain," she said.

"When I finally felt comfortable enough to tell you, I thought you would be so angry with me. And you picked my brain anyway."

"I did, didn't I?" Jen relaxed in her lounger, enjoying the sunshine on her legs and the view she thought she'd never see again. "It's so beautiful. So different than when I was here."

"When the spring flowers came, I wished so badly that you were here to see them," Ryan said. "I wished you were here for so many things."

Jen turned, resting her gaze on her. "Are you still afraid?" she asked quietly.

Ryan nodded. "Terrified."

"Can I tell you something?"

"Of course."

"I didn't know who you were," she said. "I mean, when I saw you on TV, I had no clue who Catherine Ryan-Barrett was. I don't watch entertainment shows, I don't read tabloids." She shrugged. "I rarely even go to movies. Cheryl had to tell me who you were and even then I didn't know." She reached across the small space that separated their chairs and took Ryan's hand in hers. "I don't care what your name is. That doesn't mean anything to me. You're just *Ryan*, the woman I fell in love with. Don't be afraid of this."

Ryan brought their hands up and softly kissed hers. "I don't belong in that world," she said quietly. "I don't remember a time that my mother and I ever got along, but the thing with the book separated us completely. She had no clue that writing was my passion," she said. "When my name got leaked and everyone assumed that I couldn't have possibly written the book—I mean, I must not have a brain since I'm nothing more than an heiress—my mother openly questioned it as well. She was easy pickings for any reporter who wanted a story."

Jen saw the sadness on her face but didn't comment, wanting her to finish her thoughts.

"My grandmother knew. I wrote the book while I was in college and I used to let her read it while I was working on it. She's the only one who stood by me. That's why I feel obligated to attend her annual birthday party. It's the only time I see her. See them."

"Your brother didn't know?"

"Charles' sole purpose in life is to party and to see how many women he can bed in his lifetime."

"You aren't close to him either?"

"Oh, we get along okay. He's three years older than I am. We just don't have anything in common."

"Tell me why you're a hermit," she said with a smile.

Ryan finished her beer and set the bottle down beside her chair, pausing to ruffle Kia's fur. "It started innocently enough," she said. "I wanted to escape the constant questions about the book, the reporters who were hanging around, the cameras. Being an heiress and being a lesbian, well, let's say there was always interest in who I was seen with."

"So there were lots of Megans, huh?"

"Yes. I was young, just out of college. And I needed a break. Like I said, that world wasn't for me. The only time I'd been to Aspen was for skiing, but I was familiar with it. I figured it was small enough where I could disappear for a few weeks and still provide me with what I was used to. A five-star hotel," she said with a laugh.

"I take it your tastes changed?"

"Yeah. I took up hiking. Got a dog. Nico. No matter how much money I said I'd pay, the hotel said no to dogs. So, I bought this little shack. I went up there thinking I would stay a couple of weeks, then I thought I'd stay through summer. Then the aspens turned, and I fell more in love with the place. Next thing I know, it's winter, and I'm not going anywhere. I skied nearly every day."

"Did you make friends?" she asked.

"No. I didn't want to. I didn't want anyone to know who I was. I was a ski bum, nothing more. So I fixed the shack up, thought maybe I'd stay a while. But Aspen is not some sleepy little ski town. Tourists would recognize me from time to time. My brother liked to ski Aspen so he showed up every year. It just got to be too crowded for me. When I lost Nico, I decided it was time to move on," she said. "I never once considered going back home."

"So Reese and Morgan are the first friends you've made since you left home?"

"Yes. Ten years now since I left."

Jen squeezed her hand. "Oh, Ryan. I'm so sorry."

Ryan shrugged. "It was my choice, Jen. I was used to being alone, living in my own world. This place here," she said, "is my home. I could have made it bigger. I could have bought some place closer to town. But this is what I wanted. This is all I needed." She paused, waiting until Jen looked at her. "Until I met you. Then I realized how truly empty my life was." Her gaze swept out across the mountains. "I realized that all this was nothing without you here. It had lost its beauty somehow."

"You hid it well," Jen said. "You appeared to be perfectly content with your life as it was."

"Oh, I was. But you came in and turned my world upside down. I didn't want you to leave."

Jen nodded. "I didn't want to leave."

"Why didn't you tell me?"

Jen smiled. "Why didn't you tell *me*?"

Ryan laughed. "God, I missed you." She sighed. "I missed this. Talking with you." Ryan turned to her. "How long can you stay?"

"I can stay...a while," she said cautiously, not knowing what Ryan intended. "I would love to see the aspens turn."

"It's beautiful, Jen. The mountains turn to gold. Everywhere you look, it's gold." Ryan raised an eyebrow. "They don't turn until well into September though."

Jen's heart sunk. "If that's too long, I can leave whenever—"

"No, Jen. No. I want you to stay. I just don't want you to feel that you have to. I know you've got your life back in Santa Fe. You have friends there. You have a house."

"Yes. I have all those things," Jen said. "My publisher is there. I'm familiar with it. But I don't have you there." She took a deep breath, hoping what she was about to say was something Ryan wanted to hear. "I'm crazy in love with you, Ryan. It's fireworks and Fourth of July," she said with a laugh. "I want...I want to stay." She was shocked to see dampness in Ryan's eyes. "I want to stay here."

"You'd...you'd give up all that to stay with me?"

"Yes. My heart is up here. With you." Jen knew that to be true. She'd give up everything in Santa Fe to be with Ryan. Ryan was the one who made her whole.

Ryan stood, pulling Jen into a hug. Jen clung to her, relishing the closeness she felt with Ryan.

"I want you to stay," Ryan finally said. "But I also want you to be free to leave if you want to. You know how isolated it is up here. You would get—"

Jen stopped her with a kiss, letting her lips linger, feeling Ryan's pulse spring to life. She pulled away a little, enough to look into her eyes.

"In the summer, like now, we can be in Lake City in less than thirty minutes," she said. "That's not isolated. And you have two very good friends who I happen to like very much as well. That's not isolated." She smiled. "And spending another winter up here with you, watching the snow fall on the deck, that sounds like heaven to me. That *is* isolated," she said with a laugh. "But unlike last winter, we now have something we can do," she said as her hands moved up Ryan's body, resting on her breasts, "to while away the time."

Ryan cupped her face, her mouth still smiling as she kissed her. Jen smiled too as they drew apart.

"Speaking of friends, Reese and Morgan are coming up for dinner," Jen said.

"They are?"

"Yes. Reese said you owed her a steak."

"So I do."

Jen's fingers traced the outline of Ryan's nipples, and her arousal flared. "Of course, that's still a few hours away," she said, lifting her head for a kiss.

Ryan accepted her invitation, leading her quickly back inside the cabin. Jen paused, her gaze going back to the deck, to the dogs lounging beside their chairs, then to the mountains. She smiled and let out a contented breath.

*I'm home.*

**Publications from
Bella Books, Inc.
Women. Books. Even Better Together.
P.O. Box 10543
Tallahassee, FL 32302
Phone: 800-729-4992**

**www.bellabooks.com**

**THE STRANGE PATH** by D Jordan Redhawk. Hardened by the brutal streets, Whiskey knows nothing is free. More than ever she clings to her motto: Take more than you give. But when you have nothing, anything can be tempting. It all could be a dream come true, except for the nightmares that await her if Whiskey chooses to walk the Strange Path. First in series. 978-1-59493-275-5

**FRAGMENTARY BLUE** by Erica Abbott. C.J. St. Clair's success as a police officer has brought her a new job and a fresh start with Internal Affairs in Colfax, Colorado. It's a long way from her hometown of Savannah, and among the many welcome sights on her new horizons is Alex Ryan, the head of the Detective Unit. 978-1-59493-274-8

**HIDDEN HEARTS** by Ann Roberts. With staggering student loans to repay, CC Carlson is determined to please her new employers. The first assignment as a real estate lawyer is easy: deliver an eviction notice and make it clear that it will be enforced. 978-1-59493-287-8

**DEERHAVEN PINES** by Diana McRae. The foothills of California hold many beauties—and many secrets. The walls of Deerhaven Forest Hall protect the cherished secrets of its residents, and all that they believe and have guarded for more years than they can count. 978-1-59493-288-5

**EVERYTHING PALES IN COMPARISON** by Rebecca Swartz. For the reserved Emma, life with a self-absorbed musician whom she is expected to protect is the last thing she needs. Daina Buchanan, she soon finds, is used to getting what she wants. 978-1-59493-289-2

**TATS TOO** by Layce Gardner. It seems that there are a few details about her past that Vivian has neglected to share with Lee, and the men with the big guns are back. They want what Vivian took from them: the thirty million dollar Devil's Diamond. 978-1-59493-291-5

**WRITING ON THE WALL** by Jenna Rae. It doesn't take San Francisco detective Del Mason long to realize that her new neighbor, Lola Bannon, has more baggage than a cruise ship. She's seen too many victims of domestic violence not to recognize all the signs. Their mutual spark of attraction is compelling, but she knows that for now Lola needs friends, not lovers. 978-1-59493-290-8

**SPRING TIDE** by Robbi McCoy. The waterways of the Delta tangle and weave for hundreds of miles, hiding secret coves, serene vistas and fragile depths. But they are no match for the tides of a woman's heart. 978-1-59493-292-2

**RHAPSODY** by KG MacGregor. Never before Ashley she felt so contented in the company of other women. Even so, there's always the whisper from the past. Would any of them, especially Julia Whitethorn, the charismatic, appealing owner of Rhapsody, care about her if they knew the terrible secret she's kept for twenty years?
978-1-59493-293-9

**IN THE UNLIKELY EVENT...** by Saxon Bennett. When Chase and her BFF Lacey butt heads over the Institute, she decides it's high time she prove once and for all that she is a changed woman. Her daughter, Bud, is an eight-year-old filmmaker who will document her mother's fearlessness—once she figures out how to focus past knee caps. Chase proves she can visit Urgent Care and not wash her hands afterward. She can skateboard, teach people how to drive and—to the surprise of many, including herself—she can gift wrap anything. All these changes can only lead to one thing: the Gift Wrapping National Finals.
978-1-59493-297-7

**BEING EMILY** by Rachel Gold. Emily desperately wants high school in her small Minnesota town to get better. She wants to be the woman she knows is inside, but it's not until a substitute therapist and a girl named Natalie come into her life that she believes she has a chance of actually Being Emily. A story for anyone who has ever felt that the inside and outside don't match and no one else will understand...
978-1-59493-283-0

Bella Books, Inc.

*Women. Books. Even Better Together.*

P.O. Box 10543
Tallahassee, FL 32302

Phone: 800-729-4992
**www.bellabooks.com**